THE CHAINSAW BALLET

A MIKE DUNCAVAN MYSTERY

THE CHAINSAW BALLET

THOMAS J. KEEVERS

FIVE STAR
An imprint of Thomson Gale, a part of The Thomson Corporation

Detroit • New York • San Francisco • New Haven, Conn. • Waterville, Maine • London

LIBRARY OF CONGRESS CATALOGING-IN-PUBLICATION DATA

Keevers, Thomas J.
   The chainsaw ballet / Thomas J. Keevers — 1st ed.
     p. cm.
   ISBN-13: 978-1-59414-580-3
   ISBN-10: 1-59414-580-6
   1. Private investigators—Illinois—Chicago—Fiction. 2. Chicago (Ill.)—
Fiction. 3. Nightclubs—Fiction. 4. Murder victims—Fiction. 5. Prostitution—
Fiction. I. Title.
PS3611.E35C48 2007
813'.6—dc22   2007012339

First Edition. First Printing: September 2007.

Published in 2007 in conjunction with Tekno Books and Ed Gorman.

Printed in the United States of America on permanent paper
10 9 8 7 6 5 4 3 2 1

This novel is dedicated to the fourteen police officers who conducted the raid on the Black Panther Party apartment in Chicago on December 4, 1969: courageous men whose true story will one day be told.

Raymond Broderick
Edward Carmody
John Ciszewski
William Corbett
James Davis
Joseph Gorman
Daniel Groth
Lynwood Harris
Fred Howard
Robert Hughes
George Jones
Philip Joseph
William Kelly
John Marusich

ACKNOWLEDGMENTS

Thanks to Rae, my life partner and most insightful critic.

And thanks to Sunday at the Foxtail, who has surrendered the stage for the back of the bar and is still delighting customers.

CHAPTER ONE

Though the street lamps still burned, dawn oozed through Chicago's Portage Park neighborhood, glowing faintly on the building facades, the surface of the alleys, the planes of the overflowing dumpster behind Club Belgrade which, having released its strobe lights, its pounding beat to the coming day, slumbered now in darkened neon.

But inside there was movement. Milan Krunic closed the cash register, kicked shut the door to the safe beneath, hefted the canvas bag with the evening's receipts, and moved from behind the bar to the narrow gash of front window for the second time in ten minutes. He pressed his forehead to the glass and cast his eyes impatiently in both directions.

He stood at the window half a minute more, then took a small flashlight from his back pocket and made his way into the Sarajevo room and crossed to the back door. There were no windows on this side of the club. He flipped open the lock, pressed a hip against the crash bar, cracked the door just wide enough to take in the parking lot. There were two cars there. One, the silver Mercedes, was his. Two spaces over, facing in the opposite direction, was a maroon minivan he did not recognize.

Milan decided to wait no longer. He stuffed the flashlight into his back pocket, shifted the heavy bag to his right hand, let the door shut behind him and made his way to the Mercedes, fishing the keys from a pocket and pressing the remote. *Minivan has no business here,* he thought—*neighbors take advantage.* He would again bring up to his partner the subject of hiring a towing company. *People use parking lot and never come into club—for what reason should we give to whole neighborhood free parking?* He had raised the subject once before, when his second partner, Uri, was alive, and Uri said that they should not be towing away cars that might belong to customers. Maybe customer gets lucky, Uri would say, leaves girl's car in parking lot, drives her to motel.

But Uri was dead now. Now it was just Milan and Stepan. *Minivan does not belong to customer,* he thought. *Club Belgrade patrons are young, pretty hip. Not to be caught dead in minivan.*

He opened the passenger door and swung the bag onto the seat. Hearing behind him the hum of the minivan's window coming down, a wave of heat dampened his face. He turned his head slowly, his heart drumming against his sternum. Then he caught sight of the driver, and a smile creased his face. Palm on his chest, he made a little drama of exhaling. "Why you not knock on door, come inside? You scare me like this."

The driver didn't answer.

"I was waiting for Smoot. You could have drink, wait with me. You want to come inside?"

The driver still did not answer.

"That Smoot. Probably sleeping in alley somewhere, that guy."

The driver kept his silence.

"Is something wrong?" Milan Krunic said.

Instead of answering, the driver poked a short-barreled shotgun out the window, leveled it at Milan's legs, and fired. The blast threw Milan against his car, his head striking the roof, then his butt slid to the asphalt. He braced his hands in a thickening pool of his own blood, tried to prop himself up, amazed at the volume of blood gushing from his thigh, amazed that he felt no pain. Wide eyed, he scanned the minivan. From this angle he could not see the driver, though he was pretty sure the driver's seat was empty now. Should he try crawling back to the club door? No. He remembered his cell phone, he'd left it on the console between the seats. He tried raising himself, already weak from blood loss, and then he saw the van's rear hatch rise up and he heard a kind of burping sound—what was it? It came again, and then again, and recognizing it, terror liquefied his belly. Now the chainsaw snarled to life, and the driver came around the back of the minivan holding it at high port. Revving it, he stepped on Milan's arm. Milan tried to pull his arm away, his flesh scraping asphalt, but he could not free himself. The man lowered the blade to Milan's wrist, and Milan squeezed his eyes shut, too weak to move, surprised again that he felt no pain. The blade ripped through his arm, spitting out blood and splintered bone and chunks of flesh. Milan never opened his eyes again.

CHAPTER TWO

All women are sex objects. That pearl came to me while I sat at my second-floor office window watching the stream of pedestrian traffic passing on Washington Boulevard, a diversion which often inspired the profoundest of insights into the human condition. A slender beauty breezing along the sidewalk across the street brought this one.

But as with all great truths, there are exceptions: siblings, daughters, mothers. (I don't care what Freud said, he was a sick man.) That's about it. Well, and nuns. And there are, of course, categories of women whom maybe you shouldn't regard with lust: wives of friends, for example, or friends of wives—but that doesn't mean they're not sex objects, you just try not to see them that way. Ugly women? Sex objects. Stupid women? Yep. Fat women? The same. Older women? Especially older women, with those sage creases around the eyes. Big ones, small ones, the long and the short and the tall—all sex objects. Feminists? Close, but even feminists, who can be cute when they're angry, which around me seems like all of the time. I don't get it. I *love* women, yet feminists seem to regard me as a Person in Need of Exorcism.

The woman across the street neared the corner and slowed, a waterfall of chestnut hair bouncing on her shoulders, her yellow, tailored jacket accentuating her long waist, her full breasts. Directly across from my window she stopped, waited for the light on Wells Street to change. My phone rang. I lifted the receiver.

"Legal Investigations, Mike Duncavan," said I. The woman folded her arms and tapped her foot, then snapped up her wrist to check her watch.

"Orson Prescott, Mike," the voice said. "How ya doon?"

"Orson. I'm busy as a burglar." The simile really made no sense, but I didn't particularly like Orson, and I didn't ask him how he was "doon." If he had reached my answering machine, I probably would not have returned his call. Well, maybe I would, out of curiosity. And out of the need for gainful employment. When you eat what you kill, you eat a lot of crow.

"Long time no see," he said.

"Right." I let it hang there, hoping he'd get to the point. Face it; Orson Prescott would not be calling to send me business.

"Guess you heard, I'm no longer with Piedmont Mutual."

Before I was disbarred, back in my glory days when I was a partner in a big law firm and drove a new Lexus, I did both defense and insurance coverage work for Piedmont Mutual Casualty Company, and Orson Prescott—if his parents thought the name might imbue him with a little class, the experiment failed—had been a Piedmont claims adjuster. Claims adjusters move among insurance companies like career soldiers move among Army bases—why the hell would I care if he no longer worked at Piedmont? And Orson never liked me, either. He was always whining to our managing partner about my "independent attitude." I could afford to be independent then. So why was he calling me now?

Could it be business? I turned my chair to the desk, my eye falling on a stack of unpaid bills, most of them bearing "THIRD NOTICE!" and "PAST DUE!" stamps like angry red welts. "I didn't hear that, Pres. Where you working now?"

"You ain't gonna believe it. Guess."

13

Was it really worth it? How far would I sink? The unpaid bills lingered on the fringe of my vision. "Liberty Mutual," I said. Everyone I ever knew who worked at Liberty Mutual, at least in the law department, never stopped talking about what an awful place it was.

"I'd have to be pretty desperate," he laughed. "No, I'm with a life insurance company now, Icelandic Mutual. I'm living in Minneapolis. Big switch, hah?"

Going from a casualty company to a life company *was* a big switch for a claims guy, but why did he think I cared? "Yeah, big switch," I said.

"I heard all about your problems, Mikey. Heard you're doing private investigations now."

"Right." The chestnut-haired beauty crossed Wells Street and disappeared into Starbucks.

"Well, I need someone like, with your experience. You were a homicide detective when you were on the police department, right?"

"Right."

"I got kind of a limited budget, but I figured you maybe could use a few shekels."

You're all heart, I thought. "I appreciate the sentiment, but believe it or not, Orson, lately I'm turning away more business than I keep. Probably I should hire some help."

"No kidding? What's your hourly rate?"

"A hundred an hour."

A beat. "A buck an hour? That's a little steep for a private investigator, ain't it, Mikey?"

"Plus expenses. What do you usually pay a private investigator who's been both a street cop and a trial lawyer?" I was starting to steam, and now I didn't give a rat's ass if he hung up on me.

"That's the thing, I don't know anybody with that kind of experience."

Well then, Einstein, it's your move. I waited.

"Okay, I got to clear it with my manager. Think maybe you could give me a break on your rate, for old time's sake?"

"Sorry, Orson, I don't do that. Nothing personal, it's strictly policy." His move again. He needed to check with his manager the way a car salesman needs to check with his manager. But now I was intrigued. I was doing a little investigative work for some casualty companies, but I'd never been hired by a life insurance company.

"Let me tell you about the case," he said. "We insure these three guys, partners in a nightclub, under a partnership policy? You know about partnership insurance?"

"Key man insurance?"

"Yeah," he said. "For when someone croaks, to provide funds to buy out the deceased partner's share. So they don't have to liquidate assets to pay off the family."

"Right. Or have the widow step in as their new partner. So I take it someone, ah, croaked?"

"Worse. Two of them got murdered. Not at the same time, about a year apart. Still, they're dead as doornails, and we've paid out now, a million on each. That's two million dollars."

Orson always did excel at math. "Let me just jump ahead here if you don't mind, Orson. You think the surviving partner killed these guys?"

"Maybe, maybe not. I don't think that stuff really happens except in movies, but anything's possible." He paused to emphasize what came next. "Truth is stranger than fiction, know what I mean?" He paused again to allow me to ponder his meaning. "Point is, if he didn't, then he could be next. We'd rather not pay out another million." He paused once more. "Know what I mean?"

This time I wanted to ask him to explain his meaning, but

15

instead I said, "I'm afraid I've got a pretty full plate, Orson. When will you know if you need me?"

"Shit," he said. "Okay, you're hired, a hundred an hour. Just try not to get too heavy-handed on your billing, okay? My manager hangs over my shoulder like a fuckin' buzzard. You know how insurance companies are."

"I take it that neither of the murders was solved?"

"Right, neither one. The most recent guy, he only got it like a couple weeks ago, but I don't think the cops are going anywhere with that one, either. The first one was killed about a year ago. Both cases were a little strange. The most recent one, he got it in a robbery in the parking lot of their club, after they closed. The cops think he was carrying money to his car."

"And you think there's something strange about that?"

"Well, the way they did it, they shot the guy in the legs with a shotgun, then chopped off one of his hands with a chainsaw. Guy bled to death."

He was right; not your typical robbery. Sounded more like a message delivered. "What happened to the first partner?"

"They found him sitting in his car, in front of his house, with a plastic bag over his head. He was suffocated to death."

"To death, huh?" Such a putz, I couldn't help it.

"Yeah, to death."

"Orson, these sound a lot like mob hits," I said. The reason these murders were never solved seemed obvious, and the chance of me ever solving them on my own was about nonexistent. But what the hell, Orson would be paying by the hour.

"Look, I don't know about that, that's your area. The partners are all Serbians. I mean, now two of them are dead Serbians. They owned a Serbian night club on the north side."

"What can you tell me about these guys?"

"Not much. What I got is phone numbers and contact names

from the insurance application, and the claim for benefits. That's about it."

"If there's only one partner left, why does he want the policy anymore?"

"I don't know, but as long as he pays the premium it's still in force."

"Can you fax me the documents you have? I'd like to talk to the agent who sold the policy, and the remaining partner, as soon as I can."

"Sure, but I got to tell you, the guy's not too friendly. Listen, I hope quarterly billing is all right, that's the only way the company will do it. If that's okay then I'll fax over a letter this afternoon with all the information about the case."

"I bill every month."

"That's fine, Mikey. We only pay quarterly."

CHAPTER THREE

In half an hour my fax machine was spitting out the documents Orson sent from Minnesota Mutual: insurance application, claim forms, and the death certificates. He was right, there wasn't much information there, but I got the names, dates of birth, dates of death—enough to get the police reports.

There are a number of ways to get police reports. You can order them through regular channels, but then the police department routinely blocks out so much of the information they're practically useless. You can make a formal request through the Freedom of Information Act, but that takes several weeks.

Or you can bribe a clerk. That's what I usually do. In principle I don't believe in bribery, but I make an exception when you're paying someone to give you something you have a right to have in the first place.

And sometimes when I'm in a real hurry, I call my old homicide partner, Marty Richter. On this one, I wanted to get the meter started right away. I reached Marty, a watch commander, at the station.

"Need a favor, Marty," I said. "Can you get me the reports on a couple of homicides?"

"That's not so easy anymore, Mike. Homicide reports are a special case, now. But I'll see what I can do. Cost you a double martini," he said.

"Done. Dead guys are Milan Krunic and Uri Simunic." I felt

pretty smug then, rattling off all the statistics that record keepers crave but you rarely can give them—dates of birth, dates of death, social security numbers. "It's two separate cases, one about a month ago, in the Jefferson Park district. The first one happened around a year ago, near the guy's house, in Edison Park. How about dinner tonight?"

"Can't tonight, I got a Little League meeting."

"Already?"

"Spring is in the air, Mike. It's mainly for new coaches. How about tomorrow night?"

"See you at The Old Barn at seven. How soon can you get the reports?"

"I can't promise anything, I said I'd try. If I can get them, you want me to fax them over?"

I told him that would be good and said goodbye and turned my chair to the window, to a Washington Boulevard that was starting a whole new life. Chicago's downtown was metamorphosing. By the end of the fifties, the nightspots and theaters had abandoned the area, and for three decades afterward, the Loop turned into a desert at night. But recently, the old warehouses fringing the Loop have been converted to condos, and residential buildings were springing up all over the Loop. The theater district is open again, nightlife coming back. The old Bell Telephone building across the street, which takes up most of the block, is all condos now, and a CVS Pharmacy has opened on the corner, directly across from my window. Dogs are a common sight on downtown streets, dragging their plastic-bag-toting owners behind them. It reminds me a little of Paris, without all the dog doo-doo.

Spindly trees lining the edge of the sidewalk across the street, planted only a year before, showed no signs of buds yet—spring wouldn't officially arrive for another week. But it was a warm day for March, the afternoon sun spilling orange light into the canyon of Washington Boulevard, and the secretaries on the sidewalk were mainly coatless. Spring *was* in the air, and the view from my window was beginning to improve.

I went out and grabbed a sandwich at Monk's Pub, and when I got back to the office a stack of police reports was sitting in the tray on the fax machine. Marty Richter had come through for me again. I poured a cup of coffee from a pot that had been simmering since early morning. It looked like crude oil, so I diluted it with water from the sink. It's an amenity you don't get in these fancy, new high-rises, a bathroom sink right next to your desk. Hell, those poor people can't even open their windows.

The reports were pretty meager on both homicides. I looked at Milan Krunic's first, the fresher one. Responding to a call of "shots fired" at 5:05 a.m., the beat officer found Krunic sitting slumped against the passenger door of his Mercedes in the parking lot of Club Belgrade in a "copious" pool of his own blood. He was DOA. His right hand had been cut off, but the blood had come mainly from a shotgun wound to his left thigh, a blast which severed Krunic's femoral artery.

The guy who called the police, a neighbor who heard a gunshot at about two minutes after five, said he heard what sounded like a small engine starting up. Considering the wound, the spray of blood, bone chips, and flesh chunks on the pavement, it must have been a chainsaw. A couple of other neighbors heard the gunshot, but no one could tell the police any more than that.

Krunic's Mercedes was the only car in the parking lot. The detectives taped off the scene, photographed the body, and with the help of a few patrolmen just coming onto the day watch, did a grid search of the lot. They inventoried eight cigarette butts, a penny, a smashed barrette, and an empty Trojans packet.

The weapon was a twelve-gauge shotgun firing double-O

buckshot at fairly close range—the shot cone was tight enough to deliver all nine slugs to Krunic's thigh. There was a trace of powder residue on his clothing, but no scorching. That would put the shooter about twelve feet away.

The empty shotgun shell was not found, but that didn't mean much. Only an autoloader would have spit out the shell, and anyway, the shooter could have fired from inside a vehicle. Or he could have picked up the empty shell—he surely didn't act like he was in a hurry. After he shot Krunic he must have got out his chainsaw, pull-started it, and lopped off the hand.

It most likely went down in that order: the shotgun anchored Krunic's butt to the asphalt, giving the killer time to go to work with the saw. Otherwise, it would be hard to get someone to stand still long enough to get the hand off. He must have wanted Krunic alive when he lopped it off, otherwise, why not shoot him in the head?

There could have been more than one offender, they could have held him down, but Krunic's clothing wasn't disheveled—no sign of a struggle. And the pathologist noted that there wasn't much bleeding from the amputation wound, an indication that he'd pretty much bled out by then. But why cut off the hand at all? Why would the killer take the time, the added risk, to fool with a chainsaw? It meant something to the killer. Some kind of message.

Krunic was divorced, lived in a condo on the Gold Coast. The detectives interviewed his surviving partner, Stepan Vasil, at his home in Edison Park. They noted in their report that he was "uncooperative." They asked him to come into the station the following day. He did, showed up with his lawyer, and he sat there taking the fifth on nearly every question. He did disclose that Krunic would have had the evening receipts with him, and the money was missing.

The detective asked him why they didn't use an armored car

service. He said he didn't need one. They asked him why Krunic, a principal partner, was closing the place all alone. He said, "We trust each other. No one else."

So the case was listed as a robbery/homicide, but there seemed to be very little follow-up. Routine interviews of neighborhood residents, of some regular customers, all led nowhere. Though the case wasn't very old, the Violent Crimes dicks seemed to treat it as a cold case, probably because it looked like a mob hit, and they had better fish to fry.

My foot fell asleep. I hobbled over to the coffeepot for a refill with a thousand pins sticking my ankle, caught sight of the syrupy goo clinging to the bottom and changed my mind. I rinsed out the pot in the sink, then stood a minute at the window wondering how quickly Krunic lost consciousness, whether he got to watch the saw rip through the bones of his wrist. We'd probably never know.

But someone knew.

I sat down again with the reports on the murder of the other partner, Uri Simunic, not quite a year before. Uri was found dead in the passenger seat of his car, parked in front of his house on a shady, tree-lined street in Edison Park. His head was covered with a plastic bag bound tightly around his neck with a plastic cable tie. His hands were secured behind his back, also with a cable tie. A neighbor walking his dog found him at about six a.m.

I didn't have the actual autopsy report, but a supplementary report submitted by one of the detectives paraphrased the medical examiner's findings. The autopsy confirmed that the cause of death was asphyxiation. The dicks would have noted anything else unusual about the body, anything they'd found themselves, or that the pathologist noted in his report, but besides some abrasions around the neck where the bag had been secured, there was nothing else noted. I jotted on a legal pad: get autopsy photos. The dicks would probably have noted if they'd found any sign of a struggle when they first saw the body. Still, you got to wonder if Simunic willingly submitted to having his wrists tied behind him.

Simunic left a wife, Jasmina, and a daughter who was away at college at the time of his murder. The detectives didn't get much information from the wife. On the day her husband was murdered she was hysterical, and she spoke no English, and while they were at the house Simunic's two business partners showed up. They reluctantly acted as interpreters, kept telling the detective that she didn't know anything, that they should show a little pity and leave her alone.

The detectives arranged for her to come into the station about a week later, this time to be interviewed through a Serbian interpreter. The two partners brought her in, both of them throwing their weight around. When the detectives told them they would not be allowed in the interview room, they protested, only settled down when one of the detectives threatened to lock them up.

Jasmina was reluctant to talk, answering almost every question with, "I don't know." She'd met Simunic here, in Chicago; they'd been married four years. Where did they meet? At Club Belgrade. Was Uri an owner? Yes. What was the nature of his interest in the business? "I don't know."

Since Vasil and Krunic happened to be at the station anyway, the detectives tried to interview them again. They refused to be questioned separately, but this time they talked a little more—at least more than Jasmina. They disclosed a little about their business, Club Belgrade, a nightspot on Belmont Avenue that catered to European singles. There wasn't much to tell. The three had been friends in Serbia, came over to the U.S. when the war in Bosnia was over. They pooled their money, bought the club. Both Krunic and Vasil were divorced, both had children in Serbia.

But they insisted that they had no idea who killed Uri, didn't have a clue about what could have been the motive. They were enthusiastic about one thing, though: Stepan Vasil told them, "You find out who did it, don't worry, we take care of him for you."

Afterward, the interpreter hung around and talked to the detectives, told them he thought that Jasmina was probably telling the truth—she probably didn't know very much about what her husband did. That was the way of old Europe, particularly among Jasmina's class. In the old country she would have been regarded as a peasant who'd married well. No doubt she took care of the household and was careful to stay out of Simunic's way.

The reports didn't mention anything about life insurance policies. My guess was that the detectives never brought it up. Not really much of an oversight, but I wanted to hear Vasil talk about it all the same.

I jotted on the legal pad:

- Interview Stepan Vasil.
- Talk to agent who sold insurance policy?
- Drop by the club.

Chapter Four

The following evening I arrived at The Old Barn at ten minutes to seven, spotted Marty Richter's midnight-blue Buick already there, and slipped into the space next to it. I drive an '84 Dodge Omni. It had been my first wife's car, before the divorce. I gave her my Lexus and took the Omni expecting I'd buy a new Corvette right away. I did, a brand-new, cherry-red one, but since they offered me peanuts in a trade on the Omni, I kept it. Good thing: my second wife got the Corvette.

The restaurant really once was an old barn which, over the years, gave birth to a variety of geometric additions that now clung to its flanks like a litter of suckling pigs. Known for its charm as well as its food, the rambling interior is comfortably elegant in red leather and walnut and plush carpets, lending credence to the legend that it had been a speakeasy in the twenties. In the days when I was growing up, going to Sunday dinner at The Old Barn meant a trip to the country, the building rising as it did out of a sea of cornfields. Now it squatted like a beached whale in a sea of suburban ranch homes.

I found Marty sitting at the bar, fingers laced in his lap, studying the classic form of a chilled Martini-with-olive, and climbed onto a stool. Without a word, Marty raised his glass and anointed me. "I didn't want to start without you," he said. He drank.

"But you are starting without me." I ordered a Stoli on the rocks. He asked if I'd heard from Beth, my ex; and I asked about Donna. We finished a round, ordered a second, and carried the glasses to a table.

The Old Barn features a special appetizer: Mushrooms Tomas. I would swim across Lake Michigan in January if it was the only way to a steamy plate of Mushrooms Tomas. When Beth, my first wife, and I would come here with Marty and Donna, Beth called it "heart attack on a plate," and she'd eye me reproachfully when I ordered it. If Beth would only take me back now, I'd never look at another woman again, let alone another plate of Mushrooms Tomas.

"Can I start you with an appetizer?" the waitress asked. Marty ordered a shrimp cocktail. I ordered the you-know-what.

"The reports you sent me, did you read them?" I asked Marty.

"As a matter of fact, I did. You're working for who?"

"A life insurance company. New wrinkle for me."

Marty snapped open his Zippo with the Marine Corps emblem, lit a cigarette, blinked twice in the smoke. "I thought you did most of your work for insurance companies."

"Right, casualty companies. This is a life insurance company. They paid out on the dead partners' key man life insurance—paid out twice now, a million dollars a pop."

"How many partners are left?"

"Just one."

As the waitress put down the appetizers, Marty circled our drinks with a finger. "Two more," he said to her, then he sat back and shook his head. "Insurance companies sure hate to pony up, don't they? So they think this is, what, serial suicide?"

"I don't think they have a clear idea of what to think of it, other than they've paid out a lot of money under some very strange circumstances, and don't want to have to pay out again any time soon. You can't blame them. Two out of three of their insureds, relatively young guys, kick off within a year of each other, and not from natural causes."

"I hope you're getting paid by the hour. You know as well as I do, Mike, you can dig 'til you're blue in the face and you won't come up with a whole lot on this one. These got to be mob hits. So what's the insurance company's theory?" Marty chomped off half a shrimp.

"Like I said, they don't have a theory, that's why they hired me."

He drew a napkin across his mouth. "Who got the insurance money, anyway?"

"The partnership buys the insurance so if a partner dies, they can use the proceeds to buy out his share of the business from the next of kin."

"So the insurance company thinks maybe the next of kin did it?" He stabbed another shrimp with his fork, popped it in his mouth.

I shrugged. "That's not likely. The guy who got it first, Simunic, had a wife here, but from reading the investigator's impression of her, she's not a suspect. The most recent one, Krunic, was divorced, his kids are in Serbia."

"Well, you know as well as I do, this case isn't about insurance, it's about the business. About muscle, somehow. Power." The waitress put down our drinks, and we ordered, and when the waitress took away our menus, Marty said, "I'm wondering about one thing. You said the money the dead guy was carrying was gone?"

I nodded. "It would have been in a canvas bag. But whatever the shooter's motive was, there would have been no reason not to grab it. Maybe he wanted to make it look like a robbery."

Marty was lifting the last shrimp. He shook his head, pointed the shrimp at me. "It doesn't look like a robbery, not to anyone with any brains. You maybe want to watch and see if one of the patrol officers—the first one on the scene, maybe—shows up with a new car any time soon." He chewed the shrimp.

I laughed. "I'm going to be talking to the beat officer, anyway. I'd really like to talk to the homicide guys, but I'm a little hesitant. I don't know if they'll talk to me."

Marty looked at me blankly for a few seconds, then his eyebrows lifted in a look of surprise, as they sometimes did when an idea struck him. "Hey, wait a minute," he said, "Wally Phelps, he's at Area Five Violent Crimes now. Why don't you call him?"

I had been Wally Phelps's field training officer when he started as a probationary patrolman. At the time, I had transferred back to patrol from the detective division, which worked out better for night school classes—I could work straight midnights and avoid a lot of overtime.

"I don't know, it's been a long time since I talked to him."

"How about I give him a call, sort of smooth the way?"

I nodded. "Couldn't hurt. Thanks," I said.

It was still pretty early when we said goodbye in the parking lot. Marty had Donna waiting for him at home while I, on the other hand, had only my dog, who never complained when I came home late. The Old Barn had filled me with memories of Beth, of dining there with Marty and Donna, and the drive home was full of regrets. We'd had such good times there, the four of us. Those good years: great income, stable friends, a wife who loved me.

Beth had been the best thing that ever came into my life, and I threw it away. Caught in the jaws of midlife crisis, I had craved the sowing of wild oats, the free and hungry pursuit of exotic women. No; pursuit of women of every kind—the possibilities seemed endless, time was fleeting. In a very short time all my fantasies had actually come true. Amazing, how easy it was to lure some exotic airhead between the sheets when you were a successful lawyer. Then, in an even shorter time, the novelty was gone. Though I continued to bed women of the most exotic sort, I found myself fantasizing that each of them was Beth. Yes, I do know how pathetic that sounds.

We are still friendly, Beth and I, and there are times when I think there is hope of our getting together again. That is my enduring fantasy. But infidelity had brought down our marriage, and I wasn't sure, even now, that I could remain faithful to her. Was it Woody Allen who said that God gave men two heads, one above and one below, but only enough blood to operate one at a time? Women have always been my weakness. That, and an impulsive nature when it comes to throwing a punch—a couple of traits that have helped me along life's journey like a roller skate in a blind man's path.

Chapter Five

I live in Bucktown, on the second floor of a two-story bungalow on McLean, across the street from Casimir Pulaski School, one of those old frame buildings that sits a couple of feet below the sidewalk. My landlord, Fred Havranek, is a retired fire captain who happens to love dogs, and he gives Stapler, my Llewellyn Setter, the run of the backyard.

I was just starting up the stairs to my apartment when Fred's door swung open and he stood there in an undershirt and mussed hair, looking as though he'd been napping. "Mike, you got a minute? You gotta see this." He gestured with his head, and disappeared inside.

I followed him, his apartment a museum of old fire-fighter memorabilia, to a back bedroom. He stopped inside and, beaming, pointed to the wall. "I picked it up on eBay."

Hanging on the wall was a fire ax, chromed from end to end, suspended on a walnut plaque. "Got it for a song," he said, and tapped a pale rectangle of old glue where a dedication plaque would have been. "That's probably why it was so cheap. I just wish I knew the history."

I nodded, trying to look impressed. "Really nice," I said.

He looked at me intently, without moving. "Hey, stop in now and then, will ya? Don't be such a stranger. Can I get you a Coke or something?"

"Thanks," I said. "I got to feed the dog."

I mounted the stairs feeling I hadn't handled that well, wishing I'd stayed and talked with Fred. But how much can you say about a chrome fire ax?

When I moved in, Fred's wife was still living. Widowed now about two years, Fred was undoubtedly lonely, and I opened my front door resolving that I would stop in and visit him now and then. You couldn't ask for a better landlord. He volunteered to look after Stapler whenever I was called out of town. I used to reciprocate, and on occasion look after Fred's cat, Butler. Butler was no trouble; he even tolerated Stapler in that snobbish way of cats. But then one night while I was caring for Butler, someone who thought he belonged to me hung him upside down from a light fixture outside my back door, and ripped his guts out. I thought Fred would hate me after that, but he didn't. Eventually I killed the guy who did it—maybe that squared matters for Fred.

I fed Stapler and watched TV for a while, then went to bed early, but I couldn't sleep. I kept thinking how each new case was a test I wasn't sure I was up to, that I was about to prove to the world yet again that my aptitude for failure was limitless. At eleven-thirty I got up and got dressed and decided to drop by Club Belgrade, comforting myself in the delusion that I was working day and night. Also hoping it would bring weariness, followed by sleep. I headed north on Western with lightning rippling the horizon, and when I turned onto Belmont I flipped on my windshield wipers.

The rain had stopped by the time I located the club, just east of Long on the north side of Belmont. There were only a few cars in the parking lot, and I pulled into the space where I figured Krunic's body had been found, propped against his silver Mercedes. I sat there a minute looking around, hoping for inspiration, just a small something. Nothing came.

I walked around the building to the front entrance, on the south side of the building facing Belmont. Three guys were standing in front in animated conversation, two of them looking like professional wrestlers, the third as tall as the others but slighter of build, with blond hair and a military crew cut. He wore a long, black leather trench coat. One of the wrestler-types had a foreign accent—Serbian? The other sounded pure Chicago, but trench coat's accent I couldn't catch. One of the wrestler-types smiled and nodded at me and held the door open.

The interior was dark, and I found myself looking endwise down a long bar, a large room with a dance floor off to the left, a raised DJ platform at the far side. But the music was silent, the dance floor empty.

I took a stool near the middle of the bar. Eyes shifted in my direction, eyes which would not join mine. There were two bartenders, a man at the far end, and a woman closer, oxblood hair shining under a cone of light, cherry-red blouse, black skirt. Mid-forties I guessed, a woman whom, when I was in my twenties, I would have described as having a few miles on her. But now she had fewer miles than me. The set of her face was a little hard, but she wasn't bad-looking, not at all. She came over. Her smile was friendly enough.

"What can I get you?" Her accent was Slavic, like the one wrestler.

"Stoli on the rocks," I said.

"Oh, I'm sorry, we don't have it. We have Gordon's?" Her expression asking, would you like to try it?

I was surprised that a place like this wouldn't carry Russian vodka, and she must have read my thoughts. "I mean, we usually have it, but we ran out."

I told her that would be fine, and she went to pour the vodka, and it occurred to me that the ratio of customers to employees seemed about three to one.

When she set my drink down, I said, "Is it always this quiet?"

"It's a week night," she said. "Weekends, the place is—pretty lively. Wednesday nights, too. We got a dee-jay Wednesday nights, and on weekends. This is your first time here?"

"Right, first time."

"Well, if you like to dance, come on Wednesday might. If you come on weekend, the music doesn't start until nine. Eight o'clock on Wednesday. But don't come on Monday." She smiled. "Monday, we are closed."

"And when do I come if I just want to enjoy a quiet cocktail?"

"You came at the right time." Her smile was disarming. "So. How do you happen to come to Club Belgrade?"

I took that to mean: since you're not European, and since you're old as dirt, what are you doing in a club for hip European singles?

"I live in the neighborhood, and I've been curious about the place. Just thought I'd stop in and have a look. I take it the club draws a—younger crowd?"

"Yes, but Club Belgrade is for everybody. For young people, for people who want to feel young. Young people, young at heart people."

"I'm Mike," I said.

"Eva." That smile again.

"Worked here long, Eva?"

She rested her arms on the bar, revealing an admirable cleavage, and started to say something when a guy down the bar signaled, and she walked over to him. Then she opened a small refrigerator and retrieved two bottles of beer, the light from the open door accentuating her trim waist, the shape of her hips, her high breasts. There was something about the way she handled the bottles, though, squeezing them awkwardly as she moved to set them down. Then she picked them up one at a time, popped the tops off at a bottle opener under the bar and, elbows extended awkwardly, she pressed them together again, and set them before the customer. She took some bills from the bar and went to the cash register, her movement leisurely, and I wondered if she was coming back to me, then another customer waved to her, said something in that Slavic language, and she laughed and brushed back her hair and said something in reply, like the start of a conversation, and I was sure she wasn't coming back.

But a minute later she did, moving in that unhurried way, and stood in front of me with her pretty smile once more. "So. You were asking about Club Belgrade?"

"I was just wondering if you've worked here long. Seems like a nice place."

"Almost two years, now."

"Pretty good people to work for?"

"Sure," she said.

"Stepan Vasil, he's the owner now?"

Something shadowed her face. The smile was still there, just a little stiffer. She didn't answer. I tried another tack. "Looks like you've got almost as many workers as customers."

"Slow night," she said. "But even when we have a crowd, people don't start coming in until late. These young people, they don't need sleep, I guess."

"And what about you, Eva? Is it hard to keep these hours?"

"Why, you don't think I'm young?" She pretended to be annoyed.

"A lot younger than me."

She gave me a look of mock rebuke, then said, "I guess I'm used to it. The hours, I mean."

"How about Mr. Vasil, does he come around at night?"

Wariness flickered in her eye again. She studied me. "Who is that?"

"Stepan Vasil, the owner?"

"He's ah—why do you ask about Mr. Vasil?"

I shrugged. "Just making conversation. Did I say something wrong?"

"No, of course not." She pointed at my drink. "Can I get you another one?"

"Sure," I said. She carried the empty down to a row of bottles, and I watched her scoop in fresh ice cubes and set the glass down to pour the vodka and noticed she was using only one hand. Then she looked back at me and made a small gesture with her head. I didn't comprehend, and then I realized she was looking past me, and I turned to see the blond guy in the black leather coat coming out of the vestibule. He breezed past, leaving in his wake a whiff of Jade East cologne, a brand that had been popular in the sixties. Eva leaned between two customers and whispered to him. His eyes shifted to me, then back. He was about six-two, his blond hair gelled, a face full of sharp angles. When he started in my direction again, his eyes were on me but with no particular expression. I thought he was going to say something but he didn't, just swept past again, Jade East slipping past my nose like a veil.

Eva brought my drink and I paid for it and threw down an extra five. She said thank you and she gave me another smile, but this time it could have been put there by a taxidermist, and without saying more she drifted away down the bar.

She didn't come back. I finished my drink, picked up my hat from the stool next to me, and got up to leave. I thought I'd trod pretty lightly, but still seemed to have pulled down a curtain of suspicion, and I sensed no one wanted anything to do with me, not this night. I'd have to take it slow if I was going to get anywhere, at least in the club.

But I was wrong about no one wanting anything to do with me. Leather coat and one of the wrestlers were waiting for me in the vestibule. "Just a minute," the wrestler said, but I was already out the door, pretending not to hear.

"Hey, wait." The two followed me outside. "We want to talk to you a minute," the other said, his voice neutral, neither challenging nor friendly. This one's accent was definitely German. "Forget it," I said, walking fast. They hastened to catch up, and a familiar fire, one which never in my life did me any good, ignited in my belly. I don't much like being messed with.

"Wait," he said again, and placed a restraining hand on my arm. Some internal valve sprang open and I stopped, fighting to stay cool.

This guy, the one with no accent, looked Hispanic. "You better move your hand," I told him, then added, "You really don't know who you're fucking with." Instantly regretting the last part.

He smirked, facing me now, and I wanted to take control of myself, but this greasy fuck still had his hand on my arm. Then he moved it, raised both palms in a peace gesture. A mocking peace gesture. "Okay, old-timer." He was stifling a laugh, shifting amused eyes from me to trench coat.

Bad mistake, taking his eyes off me at the very moment anger melted my brain. I planted three quick jabs to the middle of his face. His guard came up way too slow, and he staggered backwards, trying to turn away. Powering with my whole body, I landed a solid roundhouse to the side of his head, and he toppled like a felled redwood.

It had been too easy, and I spun to face leather coat, but he was just standing there holding up his hands in that sign of truce. There was no mockery in this one's eyes; rather, there was a disarming calm.

The big guy got to his feet in stages and started for me, wary now and hunched, arms extending from his body like he was about to pick up a log.

Leather coat yelled "Luis, no," and the big guy straightened, stood his ground, fury smoldering in his eyes.

Leather coat turned to me. "You're right, eh? About one thing? We don't know who we're fucking with. You are pretty tough guy, that's for sure." He laughed. "A boxer, no? Come on, we just want to talk to you, that's all. So. Why are you asking questions about Mr. Vasil?"

I took his measure. The other guy, I would have figured he'd have tied my Irish ass in a knot. I got in some lucky shots, took him by surprise. But this guy. I could take this skinny Kraut, no problem.

"Well, I don't want to talk to you," I said. I started to walk past him and he stepped in front of me, which I expected him to do, and my left snaked to his jaw—but it never got there. Quick as a cat he side-stepped, did this odd sort of pirouette, and then I was seeing stars. Real stars. Flat on my back on the sidewalk, my head throbbing, I was looking at the Milky Way. Then the other wrestler came outside and walked over to me and kicked me hard in the ribs. I rolled away, and trench coat yelled, "Tony, goddammit," and pushed him back.

And then I got to my feet slowly, and as I did, the side of the building was pulsing in red and blue light, and a squad car, followed immediately by another, pulled to the curb.

"Watcha got, Wolfy," one of the officers said, coming over.

"He was causing a disturbance inside. We ask him to leave, but he wants to fight instead."

The two officers stood facing me, brass nameplates on their leather jackets filled with light. The closest one was Smoot; the other, Oswald. Smoot, holding his eyes on mine, said to leather coat, now known as Wolfy, "You signing a complaint?"

"Sure."

The cops yanked my arms behind me, snapped cuffs on my wrists.

"Meet you in the station, then," he said.

I kept my mouth shut as they walked me to the car. No doubt someone in the club, probably Eva or the other wrestler, called the police. I knew the routine: you want to keep a liquor license, you call the cops whenever things even look like they're getting out of hand. And you are especially nice to the beat cops. Probably these coppers drank here when they were off duty, and held Mr. Vasil in high regard.

They patted me down and put me in the back of Smoot's squad. It was a cage car, the back screened like a little holding cell, bulletproof Plexiglas between the front and backseats, no door handles on the inside. Glad I wasn't wearing a gun, I took note of the car's beat number: 1634.

Driving into the station, Smoot didn't say a word. I finally said, "Look, Officer Smoot, I'm an ex-copper." Since I really did throw the first punch, there wasn't much else I could say. But Smoot's eyes went to the rearview mirror.

"Why didn't you say something back there?"

"I thought it would be prudent to keep my mouth shut."

"Where'd you work?"

"Prairie Avenue just before I left. But Area Four Homicide, mostly. It's been a while." They no longer had a separate homicide unit. Now it was covered by the catchall, Violent Crimes.

"Wolfgang, he's a pretty good guy, he likes coppers. He's trying to get on this job. Looks like you did a number on his goon, though. That might be hard to square. What kind of work you doing now?"

"I'm a private investigator."

"You left this job to be a private investigator?"

"No, I left the job to be a lawyer. I went to law school nights." I left out the part about being fired.

"Oh," he said, and I could hear his thoughts creak. "So you—gave up being a lawyer to be a private investigator?"

"Yeah, well—I was disbarred."

He shook his head. "Christ, tough break. Look, lemme talk to Wolfy. I think he just wants to sign a complaint to protect his ass. You being a lawyer and all, that might complicate things. He might be afraid of a lawsuit."

"Well, I'm not a lawyer, not anymore. And I'm not going to sue anyone."

We parked in the station parking lot, the other squad car pulling in a few spaces away, and Smoot opened the door to let me out. "I know you're gonna behave, right?" he said, and he took the cuffs off me. Walking over, the other officer frowned at Smoot, and Smoot said, "Hey, he's okay. He's an ex-copper. I'm going to talk to Wolfgang."

"Wolfy's a police fan," Oswald, the other one, said to me. Then looking at Smoot, he said, "But we got to clear everything with the tactical lieutenant, first."

"Oh, yeah, I almost forgot," Smoot said. "We got this hard-charger tactical lieutenant. This is none of his business, but he thinks it is. He's really a good guy, he's just a real tight ass sometimes. And he thinks everything involving taverns is his turf."

They shut me in an interrogation room and I sat there, just me and the bare walls and a beat map. Idly, I scanned the district's borders, traced Belmont Avenue, located Club Belgrade on the north side of Belmont. It was in beat 1634—not surprisingly, Smoot's beat. I tried to remember the name of the police officer who caught the job the morning Krunic was murdered, but I knew it wasn't Smoot. Smoot could have been off that day, or on another call—there could be any number of reasons Smoot wouldn't have handled a job on his own beat.

After about half an hour, the door swung open but nobody came in. Framed in the doorway, a trim, preppy-looking guy stood in the hall talking to the two beat officers. He had wavy blond hair, a maroon shirt open at the throat, tan Dockers and penny loafers. He seemed too young to be the tactical lieutenant, but he wore a snub-nosed .38 above his hip pocket, and from the subservient way the two were nodding their heads, I guessed he was. Then the three filed into the room. "I'm Lieutenant Verity," the guy said. "You're an ex-copper?"

"Right." The fact that he introduced himself was a good sign; cops don't introduce themselves to prisoners. On the other hand, he did not offer to shake hands.

Lieutenant Verity turned a chair backwards and sat facing me, his arms over the back. The two patrol officers remained standing. Verity had the intense blue eyes of a Moody Bible student; his physique the obvious result of hours at the gym. But up close, the crow's feet around his eyes betrayed the initial impression of youth. And I noticed that his loafers actually had pennies in them.

"I had a talk with the complainant, Wolfgang Bauer," he said. "Wolfy's an okay guy, he just tries to be real careful about the club, you know? Any trouble, they call the police." He got up quickly, animated by some internal lode of energy, and sat on the edge of the desk. "Look, I don't have to tell you, these tavern owners are between a rock and a hard place." His fingers drummed on the table. "They call too often, they got problems; they don't call enough, they got problems. But this outfit seems to run a pretty clean place."

I nodded, keeping my mouth shut, not sure where this was going. In the old days, I would have thought they were fishing for a contribution to their favorite charity, but I was pretty sure that didn't happen much anymore.

"Anyway, I think I got Wolfgang talked out of signing a complaint. And I've squared it with the watch commander. Long as no one wants to sign a complaint, we'll tear up the arrest slip." Something passed between the eyes of two the patrol officers. I gathered Verity was inflating his role here.

"Wolfgang says the bartender told you they ran out of your brand of booze, and you got a little rowdy? He says when they asked you to leave, you threw a punch?"

I shook my head. "Didn't happen," I said.

He studied me, apparently trying to decide if I really was that kind of asshole. "I believe you," he said. "But Wolfgang also said you were asking questions about the owner, whatsizname, Vasil?"

"Is that against the law?" I said, and regretted it immediately. But he took no offense.

"So that part's true then," he said. "Look, I told you I almost got the guy talked out of signing a complaint. But he wants to know why you were asking about Vasil. If you can give us some kind of explanation, I'm pretty sure he'll drop everything."

When I didn't answer right away, he got to his feet. "Listen, I'll be goddamned if I'm going to be pimping for these guys, I'm trying to help you. But if you'd rather hit the lockup, that's fine by me." I thought he was going to walk out, but he seemed to reconsider, and sat down again. "You know the owner's two partners were murdered?"

"Yeah, as a matter of fact I do."

"You do?" he looked surprised.

"Yeah, I do."

He studied me, looking as though he wanted to ask me something, but didn't. "So you can understand, right? They're wondering why the hell you're coming around asking a lot of questions about the boss." It occurred to me that the lieutenant left off, "And I'm wondering, too." As the tactical lieutenant, it wasn't his job to clear homicides, but it sure would look nice on his fitness report. I was beginning to see how Verity made Lieutenant so fast. He seemed like a very zealous guy.

"Look, Lieutenant, I'm a private investigator."

"So I'm told."

"I've been hired to look into the murders."

He stared at me a full five seconds. "Who hired you?"

Normally I wouldn't disclose a client, but this was different—the information could only benefit the client. The world takes comfort in the dubious notion that insurance companies, like banks, are citadels of legitimacy. "The insurance company," I said.

He stood again, smiling this time. "Jeez, Mike, why didn't you just say so? Okay, you're free to go." He gave me a friendly smile and for a second I thought he was going to shake my hand, but he didn't. He walked out the door, leaving me with the other two officers. Leaving me also with the knowledge that I'd been had. He must have squared everything with Wolfgang before coming in to talk to me.

But then, I'd punched out the other guy, and no one had mentioned him. "What about the other one?" I asked Smoot. "He doesn't want to sign a complaint, either?"

Smoot shrugged, ceremoniously tore the arrest slip in half, dropped it in the wastebasket. Then in a bad try for a German accent, he said, "He duss vatevah Wolfgang sess."

"Let me buy dinner," I said, reaching for my wallet.

He raised a palm. "Things have changed, Mike. Don't even think about it."

"I'm on an expense account."

He shook his head, smiling and frowning at the same time. "Quit while you're ahead."

Near the door I stopped to look at the bulletin board, at the row of faces of wanted men, and noticed a green flyer thumbtacked to the lower left corner. It was an advertisement for a benefit, for a Patrol Officer Frakes. At Poretta's, buffet and open bar, all you can eat and drink, fifty bucks. But it didn't say why Officer Frakes needed a benefit.

Then I saw Lieutenant Verity coming my way. Surprised to see me still there, he eyed the flyer. "Not to be rude," he said, reaching in front of me, tearing it down, "but they're not supposed to put this stuff up here." He crumpled it into a ball.

"What's the benefit for?"

"Frakes shot a burglar. He said the burglar pulled a gun, but they never found the gun, so Frakes is probably gonna get indicted." He held the ball of paper poised at eye level, gauged the distance to a wastebasket near the back door, and sunk the shot. "Take it easy, Mike," he said, and disappeared around a corner.

I started out the door, but an impulse stopped me. I looked around. No one was in sight. I dipped the crumpled flyer out of the wastebasket, smoothed it flat, and tacked it back up on the bulletin board.

In the parking lot the air was colder, and I zipped my jacket to the throat. I was wishing I'd asked the beat cops a few questions about Krunic. Had they been working the morning of Krunic's murder? Did they know anything about how well Club Belgrade was doing, or whether there had been any friction between the partners? Smoot had seemed friendly enough, and both squad cars were still in the lot. I decided to wait for them.

They came out a few minutes later and as they walked to their cars, I called, "Officer Smoot, can I talk to you a minute?"

Both stopped, turned to me. Smoot smiled. "Sure, what's up?"

"Were you working the morning Milan Krunic was killed?" His smile seemed to freeze on his face.

"Yeah." His eyes shifted to Oswald.

"Were you at the scene?"

"You know you can get all the reports, right?" he said. "I'll bet you've got them already. Everything you need to know is in the reports."

"What I need to know is who killed Krunic. That's not in the reports. I just have a couple of questions." His eyes went to the night sky and he compressed his lips, rolled his eyes once again toward Oswald, then he turned away and strode to his car, fishing for the keys in his pocket. "Stay out of trouble, Mike," he called over his shoulder.

The two of them got in their cars and drove out of the lot without looking back at me.

I stood there watching Smoot's taillights disappear, realizing that I had not planned this well. I had no way to get back to my car. Had I asked Smoot, he surely would have given me a lift. Surely he'd want to make conversation, and I could have steered it, with a little finesse, to Krunic's murder. Admit it, Duncavan: sometimes you're not exactly Sherlock Holmes.

I decided to hike back—a long way, but at least the rain stayed away. I made it in under an hour, and managed to retrieve my car from the parking lot without being seen by the bouncers.

Driving home, I began to wonder about Patrol Officer Frakes, the one who had shot the burglary suspect. I tended to cover over my memories of police work with a blanket of nostalgia. The need for a benefit to raise money for Frakes's defense, however, brought home that side of the job that turned me against it.

In the public's perception, the scariest part of the job is the risk of getting yourself blown away. But for me, it was the risk of *blowing somebody else away,* and getting myself indicted for manslaughter. Or even Murder One. Working homicide gave you a front-row seat to watch that risk unfold in the lives of other officers. We covered all police shootings. Not long after a copper shot somebody, an army of self-righteous, sign-wielding do-gooders went on the march, demanding vengeance, and their media counterparts lined up against the copper. Black officers were not immune, though it was much worse if you were white and the person you shot was of color.

A media frenzy would follow, the kind that made an Alabama lynching look like high tea at the Episcopalian Ladies' Auxiliary. I think they learn it in Journalism school. Coppers weren't tried in the press. Rather their guilt was assumed, and they were simply convicted. And the city powers-that-be were all too willing to distance themselves from the copper—even to make an example of him.

That's not to say that the coppers were never guilty. Maybe Frakes committed murder, maybe he didn't; or maybe it was something in between. But the fact that the burglar's gun was never found didn't mean diddly to me. If you leave the gun where it lay, as was often a copper's first instinct, it was almost bound to disappear in a hurry. I'd been there too many times, a crime scene boiling with a hostile crowd, and a host of lying "witnesses" showing up to swear they saw the whole thing.

I didn't know Officer Frakes, but I was sure I would be at his fund-raiser.

CHAPTER SIX

Mornings aren't the best part of my day. I awoke with dawn slipping in under the blinds and spreading itself like a cold surf across the blankets, the early gloom uniting with the gloom inside my head, illuminating the dark mosaic of failure that made up my life. Two ruined careers, a ruined marriage. Two ruined marriages, if you count the short, second one—but that divorce had been a blessing.

I'm the guy who inspires cautionary sermons on Sunday morning—this is what will happen to you if you don't curb your passions. Every parent should keep a poster of me on the back of a closet door, to be swung open when a child brings home a report card splattered with checkmarks for bad deportment: *this could be you someday!* My vices are principally two: A) lust; and B) an inability to count to two before taking a swing. The first one cost me my police career, then my beautiful wife. The second one I paid for with my law license.

When I was fired from the cops, I had a gilt-edged life preserver: a brand-new, night-school law degree from Kent College of Law. But good fortune, like money, is easily squandered. Lawyering fit me like a knit glove, and success came quickly. I drank deeply of the milk and honey—far too much of the honey, as things turned out. I found that women—gorgeous, sophisticated women—actually wanted to bed *me!* That brought down my marriage, to a woman with whom I am still in love—whom I still see sometimes and, pray God, I dream of marrying again someday. In my bout for success, vice "A" was the left hook, "B" the right roundhouse. I knocked myself out for the count.

Not all mornings were this bad. The soreness in my ribs, the ache in the side of my head where I'd been kicked, added something to the sweetness of the new day. I got up and brushed my teeth and went down the back stairs to the basement, pulled on the gloves and punched the heavy bag for ten minutes, then, seeing that it was past seven, worked the speed bag for another five. I had a deal with the landlord. The muted thunder of the speed bag he would tolerate only after seven. I had been a Golden Gloves runner-up—coulda binna contendah. Boxing was one thing I still hung on to, though now I just worked the bags, and little by little I could feel that slipping away.

Heart rate up, I trotted back up to my apartment, to the back bedroom which housed my weights, spent another half hour on bench presses and curls and the like, then showered, the sting of the jetting water against my skin letting me know that the world was not really such a bad place, considering the options.

Heading to the office, I drove east on Armitage in a cold spring drizzle with NPR on the radio, an angry listener whining about the duplicity of the Bush administration. I shut it off and turned my thoughts to the investigation. I hadn't been on the case a full day, and already it felt like trying to crack a bank vault with a screwdriver. Why had just the mention of Vasil aroused all that suspicion at Club Belgrade? And why did Officer Smoot suddenly clam up? He'd grown pretty friendly, once he knew I was an ex-copper. But these guys live in a world where raw power underlies everything, like a spare generator just under the surface, and their whole world lines up in a pecking order. I stopped being a comrade as soon as he saw that I wanted something from him, and was shuttled into the category of telemarketers and Jehovah's Witnesses.

But as I eased onto the southbound Kennedy ramp, a couple of thoughts merged to form an idea. Not much of one, but anyhow, an idea. One component was that Krunic and his partners were either too cheap or too proud to hire an armored car service, and Krunic was murdered as he was leaving with the receipts that morning. The other component: the workers at Club Belgrade were pretty cozy with the cops. My hunch was that Krunic had a "monthly" at Club Belgrade. I do not, of course, refer to the sort involving tampons.

Back in the days when I drove a police cruiser, a monthly was an arrangement in which some of the more entrepreneurial coppers would sometimes engage, an enterprise which the more fastidious might call graft. Though I never had a monthly of my own, it all seemed fairly harmless to me.

A businessman, almost always a tavern owner, would arrange for the beat car to be standing by when he closed—the time when he was most vulnerable to a stickup. Once a month, the beat guy would drop in and pick up an envelope—hence the name. Technically you could call it a bribe, but you could also call it a free market efficiency of which Adam Smith would have approved. The copper had to be somewhere, so what was wrong with being in a place where he might actually prevent a crime? Club Belgrade was on Smoot's beat, and Smoot was friendly with the security staff there. And for some reason, Smoot did not want to talk about the morning Krunic was murdered. There were lots of explanations for that, but I wanted to know what they were.

Assuming that Club Belgrade was Smoot's monthly—what might have happened? And why, at five o'clock in the morning, an hour when the streets are barren and the police radio as silent as a road-killed songbird—why wasn't his car assigned to the job? There were lots of possible explanations, and it really didn't matter. Except I had a hunch.

I dropped my car at the La Salle Hotel parking garage and walked the half block to my second floor office on the southwest corner of Washington and Wells. The building is small and old, some say a little seedy, but like the John Hancock and The Sears Tower, it has a name of its own: the Washington Block Building. Don't ask me why.

My office window is next to the elevated tracks that circumscribe the Loop and give it its name. I can almost reach out and touch the wheels that screech past and inspire every object in my office to dance. I happen to be on the wrong side of the tracks—outside the loop, you might say. Something oddly emblematic of my life.

I slipped the notepad from my back pocket and sat down at my desk, hoping to sketch out a plan, and saw there the notes I'd made the day before: Talk to Stepan Vasil, the surviving partner; talk to insurance agent; drop by Club Belgrade.

I crossed off the last one, then retrieved the file from the cabinet and found the number of the insurance agency—the Frimark Agency in Park Ridge.

I called the agent, Dave Donavan. Seemed like a friendly guy, said he'd be glad to talk to me whenever I wanted to drop by. I told him I'd be there in about an hour.

I try to conduct interviews face-to-face as much as possible. Using the phone is tempting, saves a hell of a lot of time, particularly when the prospect of gaining profitable information is low. But when you want people to give you every last scrap of information, there's nothing like a good face-to-face. That's when a person will drop some seemingly meaningless tidbit that can turn your head in a whole new direction.

I had a cup of coffee and paid some bills, then I put on my coat again and was on my way out the door when the phone rang. I decided to let the answering machine get it, but stood in the doorway a moment with my hand on the knob, listening to who it was.

"Mike? Are you there?" It was Beth, my ex. I charged back to my desk and snatched up the phone.

"Beth, hello, I'm here."

"Oh, hi. You okay?"

"Sure. Why wouldn't I be okay?" But I knew it was because I was talking too loud.

"You sound—I don't know."

I sank into my chair, tossed my hat on the desk, and submersed myself in the sweetness of her voice. I didn't care why she called, I only wanted to prolong the conversation. "I'm fine. How about you?"

"I'm great," she said. "More orders coming in than I can handle, but I guess I shouldn't complain about that, huh?"

Right after the divorce, Beth took a course in sculpturing small figurines. I knew at the time it was a way of coping; she'd taken the divorce pretty hard. The school put on a little show of the student's work, and Beth actually sold a few pieces. Then she got calls from people who had seen her work, and she sold a few more. Then practically overnight, she turned a hobby into a thriving business, her work selling mainly through big catalogue houses. Now her biggest problem was keeping up with the demand of an insatiable public—she was making more money than I did in my best years.

"But I wanted to ask a favor of you," she said.

I sat up. "Sure, anything."

"No, wait. It's a lot to ask, so I want you to think about it. A 'no' is perfectly acceptable, okay?"

"Sure. What?"

"Well—" I sat forward, and after a couple of seconds I realized I was holding my breath. "I'd like to borrow Stapler for a while. I'm thinking of doing a series of hunting dogs, and I'd like to, you know, observe Stapler in all of his moods. In motion and at rest, so to speak."

"He doesn't have a whole lot of moods. Happy, hungry, sleeping, that's about the gamut. But sure, you want me to drop him off?"

"That's a lot to ask," she repeated. "I don't mind coming—"

"No, no problem. When can I bring him?"

"Whenever. I'm usually here." Beth lived in Sutler's Grove, an artist's community northwest of Chicago, in a rambling old Victorian with a small carriage house in back where she'd set up her studio. "Are you sure, Mike? I know he's—" Her voice trailed off.

"He's what?" I just didn't want the conversation to end.

She took a couple of seconds. "Just that, you're so close."

"Stapler and me? I have other friends, Beth."

She bubbled with laughter, which lifted me up like a tonic. "I'm sure you do," she said. She was quiet for a few seconds, then said, "Ah, Mike? There's someone at the door. Can we continue this later?"

"Sure. When do you want me to bring Stapler?"

"I'll call you, okay?"

She said goodbye, and was gone.

I got up and went to the window basking in the afterglow of her voice. Down the street, I saw a young couple with a child coming out of the condo building across Washington. They turned my way, the man razor-haired in a leather bomber jacket, the woman in smart denim, the toddler hanging on to their hands between them. At intervals they hoisted and swung him, and I could see his little shoulders erupt in laughter. Then they stopped with their backs to me, looking at a display of cast-metal toy cars in the CVS Pharmacy window. The man turned to the woman then, smiled and said something, and she smiled back with her bright eyes welded to his, the three standing there in a universe all their own. Beth used to smile at me like that, sometimes: sudden and unguarded and absolutely loving smiles. These two people belonged to each other, and had that beautiful child between them. A dagger probed my heart: What must that be like?

I turned away and looked at the phone, wondering if I should wait for Beth to call back. She didn't say she'd call *right* back. I picked up the phone and dialed her number, then hung up before it rang. Don't be a jerk, I thought. Don't fumble. And anyway, was I ready for Beth? I didn't answer that, just put on my hat and went out to meet the insurance agent.

I got off the Kennedy at Cumberland and headed north. Park Ridge is a lovely town, and I decided to detour off the main drag and take in the parade of residential architecture for which the town is noted. If I had a family, this is the town I'd want to live in. I turned onto Touhy and located the Frimark Insurance Agency, a one-story building with a small parking lot.

The agent, Dave Donavan, ushered me into a small office, the walls covered with civic awards—Boy Scouts, the United Way, the Chamber of Commerce. His desk was stacked with files, brochures, and three-ring binders. Donavan's smile was infectious, his demeanor casual. He was the kind of guy you instantly liked.

When we sat down, he said, "I'm afraid there's not much I can tell you about these guys, except they were the kind of clients you don't forget." He leaned back and put his hands on the arms of his chair. "Unusual, to say the least. Would you like a cup of coffee, Mike?"

"No, thanks. How do you mean, 'unusual'?"

"Unfriendly. Almost hostile. Maybe that's the way they do business in Bosnia." With a sweep of his hand he said, "You see how small my office is? Well, all three of them showed up at the front desk. I was on the phone, and the receptionist asked them to have a seat. They ignored her—walked right past her and into my office and stared at me until I hung up. I didn't have enough chairs, so I invited them to step into the conference room, and one of them makes this gesture." Donavan chopped his hand sideways. "He says, 'No!' That pretty well set the tone. The three of them stood over me and fired questions like a tag team. I'd be halfway through one answer and another would fire a question. They were very wary, like they thought I was going to cheat them. I was sorely tempted to tell them to get the hell out."

I could see in Dave qualities I admired but seriously lacked, and pictured him keeping up a friendly face in spite of these jerks. I would have been down at their level in no time flat. Which is why people like me drive a 1984 Dodge Omni, and the Dave Donavans of the world get a company car and dental.

"What happened then?"

"I told them I'd get some quotes and get back to them. After I worked up the figures I called the one, Krunic, and quoted him the premium. All he had to do was say yes or no, or that he'd call me back with their decision. But he said he'd be in to see me and hung up. Couple hours later, all three show up again—no appointment, just walk right in. The receptionist asks them to have a seat, but they ignore her again, walk right into my office and stand around my desk. It was a little unnerving. I was on the phone again, and again I had to tell the person I was talking to that I'd call him back.

"They said the price was too high, and wanted to bargain with me. They just wouldn't accept that the price was the price. One of them leaned over my desk—kind of threatening—and asked what my commission was." Dave chuckled, more to himself. "I didn't tell them, of course. Finally, they just walked out. I thought I'd seen the last of them, which didn't make me all that unhappy. But they showed up the next day—all three of them again—and signed the papers."

"All coming in together like that, they sound more like the Three Stooges than responsible businessmen."

He shook his head. "Yeah, but—not exactly. I think these are very tough guys—what the hell, two of them are dead. It seemed like they didn't want to trust each other—weird way of going into business. But I'll tell you this—if there's a Serbian mafia, these guys were it."

I thanked Dave and drove back downtown, more convinced than ever that these were the sort of murders that were rarely solved.

About fifteen minutes after I was back in my office, the phone rang. "This is Wolfgang Bauer. Do you know who I am?"

"Can I call you Wolfy? All the other fellas do."

"Yes, fine," he said without humor. "Look, I got a job to do, so why don't you and I just start over."

"Okay. What's up, Wolfy?"

"I'd like to come by your office."

"Let me just check my appointment book. Looks like I've got an opening on—"

"Fuck your appointment book. I'll be there in half an hour." He hung up, bringing to mind Dave Donavan's description of his bosses' cordiality. This stuff must be in the company handbook. But what the hell could he want?

Wolfy was nothing if not prompt. Exactly half an hour later he rapped on the door twice, hard, his trademark leather trench coat a dark specter behind the frosted glass. I let him in, asked if he wanted coffee. He just shook his head, walked past me into my office, and parked himself in the chair in front of my desk.

I sat down. He slouched there in his coat, elbows on the armrests, and made a steeple of his fingers. "You and I, we know someone in common," he said. "Terry Mulcrone, used to work at Area Four Homicide. Mulcrone says you are good guy. 'That Duncavan, he's one stand-up guy,' Terry says. His exact words."

"How do you know Mulcrone?"

"I know lots of guys from the area. Lots of uniform guys, too. They come into the club a lot."

"So you came to apologize for trying to knock my brains through my ear last night?"

He sat up. "Listen, what did you expect? We tried to talk to you, and you threw a first punch, remember? Whole bunch of punches, is what I recall." He sat back, made the steeple again, and rubbed his fingers together. "Look. Mr. Vasil's partners were both murdered. No one knows why. Vasil, he could be next, and you come to the Club asking questions about him. What for?"

Apparently the police didn't tell him that I was working for the insurance company—he'd probably left the police station before they knew. So Wolfy was investigating *me*. I didn't see any reason not to lay it on the table. "I'm a private investigator. I'm investigating the murders."

"Investigating? For who?"

"The insurance company," I said.

"Oh." His eyes drifted across the carpet, back to mine. "Why didn't you just say so?"

"I think you and I share a couple of traits," I said. "I bet you don't respond kindly to being pushed around."

"So who was pushing? I was just asking you some questions."

"Listen, Wolfy, I want to talk to Vasil, so why don't you arrange it?"

He shook his head emphatically. "You don't know this guy.

He won't talk to you."

I put my foot against the desk, pushed my chair back. "Why not? What's he got to hide?"

"Mr. Vasil and his partners, they're—they're from Bosnia, they were in the war. Pretty rough, these guys."

"Yeah, but look at it this way. I want to help Vasil. I'm trying to find out who killed his partners."

"And you think you can do that?"

"The insurance company thinks so."

He shook his head again. "Don't bullshit me. You'd like to prove Vasil had something to do with the murders, wouldn't you?"

"Did he?" I watched his eyes.

His face colored. "No," he said. "No fucking way. But you don't know him. He won't cooperate with authorities. Any kind of authorities."

"You guys seem friendly enough with the cops," I said.

"Yeah, me. But not Mr. Vasil. Well, he knows how to keep the police happy." He held my eye for a second, deciding whether to say something, then leaned a little closer. "Look, you know how it goes. I mean, the guys from the Sixteenth District, they drink for half price at the club. Guys from Area Five, too. Vasil is friendly with the cops in that way. But otherwise—you don't know these Serbs. They take care of their own problems."

"And you help them with that?"

He stood, his face flushed. "What the fuck is that supposed to mean?"

I just shrugged, then waited for him to sit down, and when he did, I said, "I get the impression you'd like to get on the police department, am I right?"

"I was with military police, I worked in East Berlin. I want to get on in Chicago, yes. I took the exam, and I'm on the list, waiting, but I don't know how long they'll stay with this list."

He hesitated. "If I'm telling you more than I should, you understand why. Mulcrone says you're a stand-up guy. He thought you might know somebody that could help me."

"I don't know where he got that idea."

"He said you used to be big shot lawyer. You know a lot of important people, he says."

I didn't answer right away. "That's true," I said finally. I didn't tell him that since my fall from grace, those same important people looked the other way when I met them on the street.

"Can you help me? I hear it's really hard to get on the job now, that it takes some clout."

I didn't know if that was true or not. "Why should I help you?"

He shrugged.

I thought how much he sounded like Arnold Schwarzenegger. "I'm not making any promises. Can you get me an interview with Vasil?"

He stared. Finally he said, "I will try. But even if he agrees to see you, he will have little to say, this I much I can tell you."

CHAPTER SEVEN

I grabbed a quick sandwich at Stocks & Blondes, a hangout for stock traders around the corner, and just got back to my office when Wolfy called again. This guy seemed to be a real go-getter—he certainly worked fast. "Mr. Vasil will see you this afternoon, three o'clock, at the club." He hesitated, then emphasized: "He likes people to be on time."

I'll bet you do, too, Wolfy, I thought.

I decided to get there a little early, maybe eyeball the place for a while beforehand. I didn't know what I should be looking for, but there wasn't much to do around the office other than maybe dusting the empty desks. Ten minutes after Wolfy called, I was turning the Omni out of the Hotel LaSalle Parking Garage onto Washington Boulevard.

Club Belgrade's parking lot was empty, but I didn't pull in. The main entrance faced Belmont, with the parking lot entrance to the west of the building. There wasn't a good vantage point from which to watch both sides, so I pulled into the lot of a small strip mall across the street a little to the east, and backed into a handicapped spot where I could keep an eye on the front entrance. From here I could at least see cars entering the lot.

I didn't have to wait long. Five minutes later, a cream-colored Lexus came west on Belmont, turned into the lot, and disappeared behind the building. There was a door on that side that opened onto the lot, and I was wishing I'd taken a different position when a guy came out of the lot and walked east, beefy, middle-aged, carrying a briefcase, a breeze tousling wisps of hair from a head that was mostly bald and round as a grapefruit. He dug his free hand into the pocket of an expensive-looking leather jacket, pulled out keys. At the main door he stopped a moment, scanned up and down the street. His eye seemed to linger on my car for a moment, and I thought he'd spotted me, but his eye moved on, taking in the whole block. Then he turned, unlocked the door and went in.

Two minutes later an eastbound silver sports car slowed, turned into the lot, and half a minute later Wolfy appeared around the corner following the same routine: he looked up and down the street, then let himself in.

I drove over and parked in the lot and walked around to the front door, but before I could knock, Wolfy swung it open like he'd been waiting for me. I followed him down the length of the bar to a windowless office in a back corner. Vasil was sitting behind a desk.

"Mr. Vasil, this is Mr. Duncavan," Wolfy said.

No one asked me if I wanted to sit down, and anyway, there were no chairs. I extended my hand. Vasil waved it away irritably and looked at a handwritten note on his desk.

"Duncavan. What is that, French?" He mispronounced my name, as almost everyone does, placing the accent on the last syllable.

"Irish," I said. "It's Dun-CA-van. Like, 'Done havin'.'"

"So what do you want, Irish?"

"I want to find out who murdered your partners."

He huffed. "I have nothing to say to you."

"Look, the insurance company's paying me to investigate this. Seems to me that's a freebie for you. Unless you've got something to hide."

He was on his feet, fists on his desk, glaring at me under

59

bushy eyebrows. "Who the fuck—?" He stood there trying to burn holes through me with his eyes. I kept my eyes locked on his.

Vasil sat down then, and I glanced at Wolfy, who was staring at the floor. "Wolfgang tells me you were real police once. Otherwise we would not have this conversation." His eyes drifted to his desktop. "Fucking insurance company," he said, almost to himself, then his eyes swung back into mine. "They take your money, right? They glad to take your money, but when it's time to pay up, they don't like it, hah? Well, fuck them. They owe, they pay, that's all. That's the deal, period." His face was flushed. "And you. You are here only as courtesy, that's all, because you used to be real police."

Basking in the warmth of his hospitality, I said, "Look, you must have some idea who killed your partners. Some suspicion? Who do you think did it?"

He lurched forward, his face going from red to purple. "I *told* you, I have nothing to say to you." Then he sat back. Some of the purple subsided. "But let me warn you," he poked a finger like a small sausage at me. "I tell you this now, as courtesy also. Do not get in my way. Stay out of my business. Stay out of my club."

This cornucopia of cordiality was more than I could handle. "Mr. Vasil—that sounds so formal, may I call you Stepan? Or how's Steve?" His mouth came slightly open, but he didn't move. "Steve, let me tell *you* something. I am going to be on your ass like flies on a turd. Get used to it."

I was expecting something explosive. Instead, he leaned back in his chair and examined me a moment, and something close to a smile drifted across his face. Then his eyes flicked to Wolfgang and he gestured with his head toward the door.

"Let's go, Mike." Wolfy said, laying a hand on my arm. I looked at his hand. He took it away. We walked out together.

CHAPTER EIGHT

I took the Kennedy back downtown, wondering where the hell I was going with this. But I was steamed, wanted to get into Vasil's face now, maybe mess with his altar boys a little, piss him off just enough to let him know he wasn't dealing with somebody's weak sister. No doubt these guys played for keeps, but I was in a mood to have them show me some cards. If Vasil had anything to do with killing his partners, he wouldn't hesitate to stuff my corpse in a trunk just for laughs. Well, maybe. He knew that the cops knew that I was sniffing around, and if he *was* involved in the murders, he didn't need one more body to help the cops connect all the dots. Unless he thought there was no other way.

But wanting to mess with Vasil was an unhealthy impulse of the sort I'd spent my life trying to overcome, an appetite which eased me toward life goals like a spoonful of sand in the breach of a semiautomatic pistol. I told myself that it wasn't personal. Forget about messing with Vasil. So my ribs still ached where that bodybuilder kicked me; so what? Stay away from the club, I told myself. Look elsewhere. Make this your mantra: *This Is Not About You.*

They say a mantra is a lot like hypnosis: sometimes it works, sometimes it doesn't. At a quarter after ten that evening I found myself pulling into the Club Belgrade parking lot. It being Wednesday, the lot was full, and I drove through the alley to a side street, parked, and walked back, the thump of dance music reaching me half a block away, and as I drew closer I saw the purple strobe from the narrow window splashing onto the sidewalk. In the vestibule Luis, the bouncer I'd decked, stood smiling, checking ID's. He turned to me, without recognition at first.

"I'm old enough," I said, easing past him.

The smile fell from his face. He stepped in front of me. "You're not allowed in."

"Sure I am."

I started to go around him. He lifted an uncertain hand, but he let it hover halfway to my shoulder. I gave him a big smile and went inside.

The place was packed, the dance floor a storm of plunging bodies, every space filled with noise and pulsing light. The bar was packed, too, standers shouting in what must have been Serbian, and I squeezed between them until I spotted a single empty stool and took it. Eva was working nearby, bent to some task under the bar, and when she looked over her shoulder at me she actually did a double take. Or a two-and-a-half take, because she looked away then, and made it a point not to look back. I waved at her, trying to signal for a drink, but she pretended not to notice—easy enough to do because the place was a madhouse. But then the guy to my right signaled to her, and when she still refused to look, he said to me, "Don't worry," and he and his buddy sang out in chorus, "E-va!"

She turned, her eyes ricocheting off mine to theirs. She came over, stood in front of the guy next to me, keeping her eyes welded on him. He ordered. When she turned again in my direction I gave her a big, goofy grin and said, "Can I have a drink, too?" She stifled a laugh, then it bubbled out of her and she pressed a knuckle to her lip. Now she leaned close to my ear. I could smell her shampoo.

"You are not supposed to be in here," she said. It was a tone the nuns often took with me at St. Raphael's Grammar School.

"I'd like a drink anyway," I said, turning to meet her face, her lips close to mine, and she pulled back, eyes half exasperated, half playful. "Double Stoli on the rocks. If you're not out of Stoli."

Her eyes gradually released mine and she moved away. I watched her make three drinks. She carried two of them with her elbows out in that awkward way, and set them down in front of the guys to my right. That's when I noticed it, her prosthetic hand. She went back, retrieved my drink, and when she set it down the guy next to me poked a finger on a stack of bills and made some kind of a joke in Serbian.

Eva laughed and said to him in English, "He's no friend of mine." Then she said to me, "Your pal here just bought you a drink."

I said thank you, raised my glass in appreciation, and drank. When I put it down, Eva was gone.

The two guys returned to their own conversation, and I sat there for the next hour trading rounds with them, but otherwise drank alone, and maybe too much. I wanted to keep those guys around, possible witnesses. Who knew what could happen? Their loyalties would probably lean toward the club, but it still couldn't hurt. Eventually they left, though, and the music stopped, and the dance floor grew barren as Oak Street Beach in February. There was just me and one other guy left at the bar. Then Wolfgang came over, his flunky, Luis, following behind.

"You're putting me in an awkward position," he said.

"Really? I'm just sitting here minding my own business. Can I buy you guys a drink?"

"The boss doesn't want you in here," he said.

"I know, he already told me, remember?" Luis was hanging behind his shoulder with a theatrical frown on his face.

"Mike, I don't want to be your enemy. What do you want?"

"You know what I want. I want to find out who killed the partners. Shouldn't that make us allies?"

He didn't say anything, just tried to stare me down. Then he said, "We're closing, you got to go now." He walked back to the front vestibule, Luis in tow.

Eva, now the only bartender, was getting a drink for the only other customer. When she set it down in front of him I called to her. "I'll have one more." She was about thirty feet away, and she came over like she was on a mission. "We are now closed," she said sternly. But I could tell she was trying not to smile. I said, "Good, I'll buy you breakfast."

She looked at me with her head cocked, like she was actually thinking it over, then the smile broke through. "Okay," she said. I hid my surprise—see what you might miss out on, when you don't ask? She glanced toward the door, then back. She leaned close. "I'll meet you someplace. You tell me where. But I live in Des Plaines."

Des Plaines was a long way, and I had to think. Then I said, "You know a restaurant in Park Ridge? The Pickwick?"

She nodded. "Next to the Pickwick theater."

"Say, forty-five minutes?"

"Make it an hour," she whispered. "But listen. I don't want anyone to know."

I said goodnight to Wolfy and Luis in the lobby. They didn't answer, just watched me leave.

CHAPTER NINE

I drove to the Pickwick wondering why Eva agreed to meet me. She might have been attracted to me, but it seemed hard to believe, a guy as over-the-hill and threadbare as me. But then she wasn't exactly the freshest rose in the bunch, either. Though she was damned good-looking.

At one a.m. the Pickwick was nearly deserted, and I took a booth at the back next to the window, pleased to see that the menu listed cocktails. Then it occurred to me that I was probably past my limit. I debated having one more, decided not to, and then Eva was dropping her purse into the booth across from me, sliding in, a movement that accentuated her slender form, the fullness of her breasts. But in this light, the set of her mouth, the lines around her eyes, gave a measure of weariness to her face.

"I could use a drink." She pulled a pack of Pall Malls and a Bic lighter from her purse, lit a cigarette.

The waiter came over. "Stoli on the rocks," she said, looking at me. "And he'll have the same." Then as the waiter turned to go she said, "Bring me two of those, okay? Save you a trip." When he was gone, she said, "They say people who drink straight vodka are either alcoholics or are about to become alcoholics. You ought to know—is it true?" She picked a speck of tobacco from her tongue.

"You're asking me if I'm an alcoholic? I dunno—they say the alkey's always the last to know. I know I drink too much. But I rarely drink before five o'clock. Well, now and then I'll have a cocktail at lunch. But I almost never get hangovers."

She smiled. "Sounds a lot like me. But I don't drink too much. So," she said, settling into her seat. "I know a lot about you. You're a private investigator, a used-to-be cop, used-to-be lawyer. Also, a Golden Gloves champion, I'm told."

I shook my head. "Never a champ. And that was a very long time ago. Word sure gets around, doesn't it?"

"I know you beat up Luis. Luis is a professional wrestler, or used to be one. You must—rehearse."

"Rehearse?"

"Okay, so my English isn't so good. Rehearse, practice, work out, whatever boxers do."

I shook my head. "I do work out every day, but I couldn't spar anymore, even if I wanted to."

"Because you got shot in the ankle, right? Wolfy told me. He says you killed a guy in a gun fight."

This was getting uncomfortable. She was turning tables, with me becoming the one investigated. Wolfy had made it his business to learn everything he could about me. He'd learned a lot, and now I did not like the direction the conversation was taking. Worse, if Eva was harboring some fascination for me, it seemed to be for all the wrong reasons—I probably wasn't the person she thought I was.

But then, it might not hurt to keep her interested.

On the other hand, she could have been sent by Wolfgang. Or by Vasil himself.

"It wasn't like it sounds," I said. "It was all pretty sordid. Do you mind if we change the subject?"

"So modest," she said. She took a long draw on her vodka. "You know, Wolfy and Luis, they hassle you because they're just doing their job, but I think they really like you."

"Luis? The guy who was with him tonight?"

"Yes, Luis, too, both of them. Those guys. In their world being a tough guy is—what counts." She nodded to herself, approving her choice of words. "I don't know, it's all backwards, isn't it? Sometimes I think they enjoy pain."

"Well, I don't. I learned to box when I was a kid because my old man forced me to, and I only got to be good because I was terrified of getting the crap beat out of me." And I thought to myself: if that's true, you sure invite a lot of pain. My ribs were still hurting.

"You talk like a poet," she said, leading me to wonder what kind of poetry she liked. Then her forehead knotted, a reflection of the doubt she probably saw in my face. "I just mean, you seem kind of—sensitive. I guess you really are different from those guys."

"Why should I be anything like those guys?"

She shrugged. "Your lot in life, it's kind of the same."

Lot in life? I was about to ask her what that meant, then she said, "I shouldn't lump all of you together in the same pot of stew, should I? You're really not like them, I guess. They're not even like each other. Luis is a really sweet guy, would you believe it? Dumb, but sweet. He idolizes Wolfgang, follows him around like a puppy dog."

"And Wolfgang?"

"He's hard to figure. He was a policeman, you know, in East Berlin, before the wall came down. He is so loyal to the bosses. Boss, now," she corrected. "I think he blames himself for not saving them."

"Was he anywhere around when they were killed?"

"No, that's the thing. The bosses always locked up alone, Wolfy was never there then. He's in charge of the bouncers, he was not hired to protect the owners. But Wolfy tends to see himself as more important than he really is. And he idolizes Stepan Vasil the way Luis idolizes Wolfy. And Stepan treats

Wolfy like shit."

"Do they really need three bouncers?"

"No, usually Tony works at Demon Lover. Now there's a mean one, Tony. That's a guy who likes to hurt people." She smiled. "You're not like him at all. See? I shouldn't put everyone in the same basket."

"Or pot of stew," I said. "What is Demon Lover?"

She took her drink in both hands and stared into it. I thought she was ignoring me, and then she lifted one shoulder and said, "It's a club. Another club where Tony works, I guess. I don't know, I just heard him speak of it." Her whole body, the way she held herself, told me she was lying. I'd hit on something, and though I wasn't sure what it was, I decided not to push it. Sometimes it's like fly fishing: When you hook a big trout and your tippet's thinner than a hair, you don't want to muscle it.

"Tell me about the partners," I said.

She shrugged. "They're businessmen, what is there to tell?"

A lot, I thought. Coming out of the war in Bosnia, they were not your typical MBA-toting entrepreneurs. "You don't have any idea who might have had a motive to kill them?"

Her eyes lifted into mine. "No one knows." She leaned back, fingering her glass. "You think Stepan had something to do with it, don't you? But I know he couldn't have."

"You seem pretty sure of yourself."

"As sure as you can be about anyone." She knocked back the remains of her glass, reached for the second one.

"You know him well?" I asked.

"I know that his partners were like his brothers. And I think that he's scared shitless he's going to be next. I also know—" She fought back a smile. "At first, they wondered if you had anything to do with it." She tilted the glass to her lips, drank deeply.

"Me? Just because I asked some questions about Stepan?"

"I know, but can't you see? They're all so paranoid." Her eyes scanned the room in search of the waiter.

"Come on. They must have some idea why it happened. Someone muscling into the business. Something. An inkling of what it was about, at least."

She shook her head, stirred the vodka with a finger, then sucked her finger. "No, that's why they're so paranoid. Anyhow, the business isn't doing good. Remember what you said, the first night you came in? 'More workers than customers,' something like that. You had it right. Ends are not meeting." A thought crinkled the corners of her eyes. "You asked for Stoli, and we were out of it, remember? A place like that runs out of Stoli, that should tell you something."

Eva was showing no interest in eating, but I was hungry. "Would you like to order?" I said.

"I'd like another drink." I didn't see the waiter, so I signaled the cashier, who went into the kitchen to get him. When he came over, Eva ordered a double. I said I was fine.

"I watch people drink all night, now it's my turn," she said.

"Sounds like you knew the partners pretty well," I said. "So tell me, what were they like?"

She stirred the ice cubes in her empty glass with her finger, sucked it again. "They were each one different." She turned inward then, and whatever she saw inside her head must not have been pleasant. When the waiter came with her drink, Eva took it from him before he put it down, and knocked back a slug. When she looked at me again, an angry sheen glowed in her face.

"Actually, they're bastards, all of them," she said, as if they were all still alive. "Vasil, he's the nicest. And no, he really is not a nice man. That should give you some idea of what shits they all are. Were." She sipped. "Fuckers," she said, more to herself than to me. Her mood had changed and she slouched, idly poking at her ice cubes, lost in private thoughts. I let the silence go on. Then she polished off the remains of her vodka, held up the empty glass for the waiter to bring her another.

"You want to talk about it?" I asked.

She sat up straight, looked at me a moment, then her eyes unhooked from mine and went to the wall behind me. "No." She lowered her head again. "Look, don't ever, ever tell anyone I talked to you, okay?"

I put a hand on her wrist. "Guaranteed," I said.

"It's important," she said.

"No worries."

"Let's eat, please," she said, as if it were a chore she wanted to get behind us.

We ordered, and when the waiter took away the menus, I said, "Eva, you can trust me. I get the feeling you'd like to talk about the—the situation."

She just shook her head. When the waiter brought our food, she fell on it as though it was a last meal, not saying a word until the waiter picked up the empty plates. Then she forced a smile. "Sorry," she said. "Guess I'm not the best company tonight."

I handed her my card, then on an impulse took it back, scribbled my home phone number on the reverse side. "I want to see you again," I said.

She raised her shoulders in an exaggerated shrug. "I could lose my job," she said. Then she dug in her purse, took out a cash register receipt, scribbled an address and phone number on it, and handed it to me.

"Please, please don't come into the club looking for me. Better if you contact me at home," she said.

I walked her to her car. She stood there a moment with the door open. I resisted the impulse to kiss her, reminding myself that I was working. But then her hand snaked to the back of my head, her breasts rising against me, and she pulled my face to hers and kissed me deeply. Then without another word, she got into her car and drove off.

I watched her go, struck once more by that exceptional body throwing off pheromones like clouds of perfume. And I tried not to think about the hazards of mixing business with pleasure.

Since there was little traffic at that hour, I decided to take Northwest Highway into the city, rather than driving over to the Kennedy. Eva, I thought, had the kind of allure that never comes through in a photograph. Not a great face, but the way her body was put together, the way she moved it—it got your attention.

And the missing hand took none of that away, though it did bring to mind Krunic's chainsaw surgery the night he was murdered. Any connection between the two seemed a bit of a reach, but it made me want to know how she'd lost hers. Not the sort of thing you just come out and ask. But it was the sort of thing a woman would tell you eventually, if you got to know her better. No doubt about it: it was my duty to get to know Eva better.

I merged onto southbound Milwaukee Avenue wondering about the other place she'd mentioned: Demon Lover? If she hadn't clammed up and tried to cover her tracks, I probably wouldn't have given it a second thought. Tony usually worked at Demon Lover, she said. Impression: same job, different location. Then she made it sound as though Tony had a part-time gig of his own, somewhere else. When I asked her what Demon Lover was, why did she have to think about it?

Back in my apartment, I pulled out the Chicago Yellow Pages and searched for a tavern, a club, a restaurant—anything named Demon Lover. Nothing. Then I called directory assistance, checked all the suburbs. No luck there, either. When I put the

Yellow Pages back I noticed that the message light on my answering machine was blinking, and hit the button.

"I talked to Wally Phelps," Marty Richter said. "He'd be glad to talk to you." He relayed the number at Area Five and said, "Have fun milking the shit out of this one."

I slumped into my living-room easy chair. Stapler came over, plopped himself down across my bare feet. I tried to think of excuses not to call Wally.

Wally had showed up at the station that first night eager to go out and save the world, his black leather gear shiny and new, his cheeks full of rosy idealism. Phelps was kind of a Boy Scout, everybody's Kid Next Door. I had to force him to stop calling me "Sir." For some reason that I never understood—not then, not now—Wally seemed to idolize me. He bubbled over with delight if I called him at home, and if I asked him to stop for a drink after work, his face would almost split with glee. He never worked at being cool. Phelps was the kind of kid who wasn't cut out to play poker.

As his field training officer, I was expected to be a role model—that seems like one of God's little jokes. Here is what *Random House Webster's College Dictionary* says about the word "model": "a standard or example for imitation or comparison." And here is what it says about "role": "a part or character played by an actor."

What kind of role model was I? This is the behavior I displayed for Wally's emulation: Off duty one night, having sneaked away from hearth and loving spouse, I was caught by a man whose wife I had been porking regularly, skulking near his home. Sometimes that plays as a comic scenario, but not this time. He was wearing a ski mask and he started shooting—hit me twice. I shot and killed him. It happened in seconds, with no time for reflection. I shot to death a man whom I had befriended, whom up until that moment, I'd only been cuckolding.

I have always wanted to think that if he hadn't surprised me that way, bounding from the shadows, blazing away—if I'd only known it was him, I'd like to believe that I'd have stood there and taken it like a man. But he missed me with the first two shots, and as he continued to empty his pistol, I started emptying mine. The first bullet hit me through the—yes, it's true—left lover's handle; the second shattered my ankle and changed my life. I can no longer run, I still limp when my ankle gets tired. I put four bullets neatly in the center of his chest. He was dead before he hit the ground.

The investigation that followed closed with the conclusion that I'd acted in self-defense. So I wasn't prosecuted, just fired from the police department in disgrace.

How's that for a role model? Now I couldn't remember the last time I'd spoken to Wally Phelps, and didn't relish the notion of calling him. I went to bed, unsure whether I ever would.

CHAPTER TEN

Later that night, a couple of miles away on Milwaukee Avenue, a man named Bruno Malik sat in his darkened tavern at the end of the bar, looking out the front door, which he had propped open to give the place some air. A shot of Jack Daniels and a glass of Miller Genuine Draft sat on the bar in front of him, untouched. He felt the weight of his body pressing down on the stool, pressing onto the foundation of the building, onto the core of the earth, as if the muscle and sinew and bone that were him could turn to stone. It was not an unpleasant thought. Bruno considered how he could look up at a statue, say the one of Casimir Pulaski in the park, a statue that his father, when he'd come from Poland a generation before, had looked up at. And that statue, today, was exactly the same as when his father looked at it. He and his father could just as well be standing there together, looking at that statue. Or any statue. No matter what the statue was, no matter what the pose, the statue was the same forever—at rest and untortured by the world.

Bruno had grown up in the apartment above the tavern, had shared with his two brothers the back bedroom in which his seven-year-old, Cindy, now slept. The same room in which Bruno's two older boys had slept, now grown up and raising their own families.

But Bruno could not sleep. He had been plagued by insomnia for as long as he remembered. And it had grown worse, because he was sure now that Cindy was not his child. He knew it, and he could not sleep for thinking about it. The more Eleanor protested, the more he knew the plain truth: Cindy was not his daughter. Bruno's eyes were brown, and so had been his hair, before it turned gray. His Polish wife's eyes and hair were the same as his. But Cindy's eyes were emerald green, and her hair red as a flame, and anyone who looked at her knew instantly, and every time Bruno saw someone looking at Cindy, he felt a stab of mockery like the blade of a sword in his gut.

A bus ambled past the door on Milwaukee Avenue. Bruno picked up the shot glass, knocked it back, then lifted the beer and drank it down, waited for the fire to burn the demons from his head. But it seemed no longer to work. Now it seemed only to compress the plane of his vision, so that the entire focus of his life was no wider than the frame of the open front door.

Bruno picked up the empty glasses and carried them to the back of the bar, but he did not refill them, not this time. He put them in the sink, then reached into the space under the cash register and took out his revolver and carried it back to the stool. He laid it on the bar in front of him, its chrome surface seeming to suck the cold light from the room. He stared at it for a long time. Then he picked it up and flipped open the cylinder, dumped out the six .38 Special bullets, and set them in a line on the bar, silhouettes in the meager light like little toy soldiers standing at attention. He chose one, put it in a chamber, spun the cylinder, and snapped it shut. Then he slipped the barrel into his mouth, the steel cold against his lips, and pulled the trigger.

CHAPTER ELEVEN

A few days later as I drove to the office, WBBM news was carrying a story about the body of a woman found in a shallow grave in a Cook County forest preserve. The police thought she'd been dead almost two years, but what made me sit up and listen was the fact that she had a plastic bag secured tightly over her head.

I left the car at the garage, picked up a *Tribune* at the CVS Pharmacy across from my office, and when I reached my desk, opened it and found the story. The body had been discovered by a woman who'd been horseback riding in the early morning hours, her dog trailing along behind. When she noticed that the dog was no longer with her, she turned her horse back up the trail and spotted the dog about fifty feet into the woods, digging a hole. She called to him, but at first he refused to come. When he did come romping back, he was carrying the bones of a human foot in his mouth.

Later, the police unearthed the whole skeleton. Except for the foot, it was still pretty much intact. It was fully clothed— and the hands were bound together with a cable tie. It was the same M.O. the killer used on Uri Simunic. Not a common method of committing murder.

The article gave the location as Spring Creek Valley Preserve, which I had never heard of. I put on a pot of coffee, pulled out a Chicagoland map, and located the forest preserve in the northwest corner of Cook County. It was a huge tract of land, perhaps ten square miles, which lay hard up against the border with Lake County.

Nothing pressing at the moment, I drank a cup of coffee, reclaimed my car from the Hotel LaSalle parking garage, and headed out the Kennedy to the Northwest toll way, then turned north onto Route 59 and found myself in a different world. This was horse country, green pastures and white fences rolling into the distance. But while the map showed Spring Creek Valley as a public forest preserve, access seemed denied. The road ran past fabulous horse farms that backed up against the preserve, with no way to get to it without trespassing. At one point along the road, I did see what appeared to be a public footpath leading into the preserve, but it was flanked with "No Parking" signs up and down the road. I pulled onto the shoulder, studied the map once more. It showed a public road dissecting the preserve from east to west, but I couldn't find it.

I drove on, circling the entire expanse, and finally located what *had been* the road. It was now closed, with a brick wall across it. I nosed my car up against the wall and left it there.

I started down the road, or what was left of it, on foot, its fading, double yellow line still leading straight as an arrow into the woods. But nature was reclaiming her own, and now the road tunneled through overarching trees, edged by blankets of sod and weeds that reached toward the center of the asphalt. There were occasional horse droppings, but no other sign of human visitors. Somehow, the horsy set seemed to have appropriated Spring Creek Valley Preserve for its very own.

I walked the entire length, to the highway at the far end of the road, about a mile and a half distant. Having found no evidence of a crime scene, I started back. This time I detoured onto a path into the woods, found them crisscrossed with a maze of paths. I took one which led out of the woods and across a meadow, then coming over a hill I surprised a doe and a fawn grazing there. Ten minutes later I was thoroughly lost, and much later, coming back to the old road again, still had not found the yellow plastic tape which would have marked a crime scene. Not that the police, if they were still around, would have let me onto the scene anyhow, but I could have gotten a general idea of the setting, and maybe an opportunity to talk to them. Finally, I gave up on finding it.

Driving back to the office, the whole exercise seeming like another bust, it did occur to me that Spring Creek Forest Preserve was the perfect place to dump a body—a vast tract of fields and forest visited by only a handful of people, and people who probably never got off their horses. The Chicago police would not likely be part of the investigation, since the preserve was under County jurisdiction. I wondered: would anyone connect this murder to Simunic's?

That evening the six o'clock news carried a brief story of the murder with some video of the scene, news crews having apparently found the scene when I couldn't. A sheriff's detective said they believed the victim was in her early twenties. Though she was fully clothed, she had no identification.

I shut off the TV, knowing now that I had no choice: I had to call Wally Phelps.

I called him from my office first thing the following morning, his voice full of that delight I remembered. "Mike, what you been up to?" Then without waiting for an answer he said, "I hear you're a big-time lawyer, now."

It took me by surprise. I'd assumed Marty had filled him in on the crashing and burning of my life. "No, not anymore. I'm a private investigator, now."

"Oh." In the silence, I thought I heard the sound of computation.

"Long story," I said.

"Hey, I'd love to hear about it, man. Why don't you drop by the Area? Can you come over now?"

I told him I'd be right over.

Wally's hairline was retreating, exposing a shiny dome with a laurel leaf of black hair remaining above his ears. He still displayed that open-faced, almost childlike way I remembered. Now, I was sure, it was just a veneer covering a tough and savvy core, and no doubt served him well.

We walked back to a small office, just a cubicle with a single window that looked out on Western Avenue. He didn't ask me about the bell curve of my life's progress, no doubt wanting to spare my feelings. "Marty Richter told me you were working on the Club Belgrade murders," he said. "I don't know why, I just assumed it was something you were doing as a lawyer. Anyway, it's not my case. I did pull the files, though—I squared it first with the team that's handling it, Dalton and O'Toole. They're okay with your looking at it."

"Thanks," I said, not wanting to tell him I already had all the reports. "You think Dalton and O'Toole would talk to me?"

Wally's hand twitched on the table, an ambiguous, halfhearted gesture. "I could talk to them," he said, but from the shift of his eyes I knew it would be awkward.

"Never mind," I said. "Listen, there was a woman's body found in a forest preserve near Barrington yesterday, Wally. With a plastic bag over her head, just like Simunic."

"Yeah, they think she was murdered about a year ago."

"That would be right around the time Simunic got it. Similar M.O., too. You're working on this one, then?"

"Not exactly. It's a sheriff's case, but we're keeping in touch. They can't get any prints, the body's too far gone to get anything usable, and so far they haven't been able to match her with any missing persons. Not much to go on at this point, until they can identify the body." He kept saying "they," not "we." With unsolved mysteries, homicide liked to keep the jurisdictional boundaries brightly lit, making sure the press could see the ball was in the other jurisdiction's court.

"Mind if I keep in touch, maybe check in now and then?"

He grinned. "I hope you will, Mike. It's been too long."

At home that night I was feeling pretty good about seeing Wally again. As far as making progress on the case, I felt like I was digging a trench with a teaspoon, but I still couldn't have recruited a better ally. I watched the six o'clock news, then shut off the TV remembering that Officer Frakes's fund-raiser was this evening. I drove over to Poretta's on Central Avenue.

CHAPTER TWELVE

Poretta's parking lot was overflowing, and so were the side streets. I had to park two blocks away, on Waveland.

Inside the front door I counted out fifty dollars to a guy sitting behind a card table. He stamped the back of my hand, and I paused in the doorway of the banquet room, scanned the crowd for a familiar face. The room was full of round tables with white tablecloths, most of them unoccupied, the crowd gathered in little knots of conversation around the perimeter. On one side of the room was a buffet laden with food: no waiting. On the other side was a long bar: plenty of waiting, the crowd four deep, the bartenders laboring to keep up. Then I spotted Wolfgang Bauer across the room, in animated conversation with a couple of other men. I thought he was too far away to notice me, but when he looked my way he stared a minute, then nodded without smiling. I nodded back, and just then caught sight of Lieutenant Verity waiting his turn at the bar. I was about to walk over to him when a tall guy in a yellow sport shirt separated himself from a group of men in the lobby and came over to me. His physique was imposing: tall and lean as a pro basketball player. He stuck out his hand. "Ernie Frakes," he said with a juggle of his Adam's apple. "Thanks for coming."

"Mike Duncavan," I said.

"Sorry, I can't think of where I know you from, Mike. Not Sixteen, is it?"

I shook my head. "I worked out of Homicide, a long time

ago, on the west side."

Frakes smile was blank. Under thirty, he probably never heard of a unit called Homicide except on television, and might have thought I was an imposter.

"What's now Violent Crimes," I said. "Before your time."

Just then I spotted another familiar face at the exact moment he spotted me. I was not sure what to expect from Officer Oswald, but he came over and pumped my hand. "Mike, really nice of you to come, man."

"I see Lieutenant Verity's here," I said. "In my day, I don't think any brass would have showed up."

"There's some other lieutenants and captains here," Oswald said. "But Verity, he's very loyal to his men."

Frakes nodded. "Verity's a prince. Stand-up guy."

"Just—kind of an odd duck," Oswald clarified.

"I don't care, Earl. Yeah, he can be a pain in the ass, but he'll stand up for you, take the heat if he has to." Frakes turned to me. "Mike, why don't you get yourself a drink?"

I said thanks and headed for the bar. I really wanted a drink, but the crowd had grown even deeper, the bartenders frenetic as characters in a silent movie. Then Verity turned away from the bar with four long necks bunched in two hands, and spotted me.

"Jeez, Mike Duncavan," he said. "Sorry I can't shake your hand. You want a beer?" Before I could answer he said, "Come on over to the table, I got extras."

I followed him, pleased that he remembered my name, to a table where one other guy was sitting. Verity introduced me to Emil Zucco, a sergeant from vice. "Mike used to be on the job, worked homicide."

"Must have been a while ago, huh?" Zucco shook my hand. He was middle-aged, balding, pudgy in a plaid sport coat that was too small for him, white shirt open at the throat. We played "did-you-know" for a while, got no hits. It was too long ago.

Then Verity gestured with his head toward Frakes, still standing in the vestibule head and shoulders above the crowd. "Fucking shame," he said. "Frakes is your ideal copper. Smart, aggressive. And above all, he's a really compassionate guy. Sensitive guy. Now he could go to the slammer."

Compassionate? Sensitive? It seemed an unnatural observation for one copper to make about another. Not that cops didn't show a little empathy now and then, they just didn't talk about it, and it seemed to say as much about Verity as it did about Frakes. "Were you working when it happened, Lieutenant?"

"It's Hank, Mike. No, it happened on the midnights, I was working afternoons then. But my tac guys sure worked their butts off, trying to turn up the gun. The dead guy had a gun, all right. A stoolie told one of my guys that somebody picked it up at the scene and took off with it, right after the shooting. But we haven't been able to track the story down, not to mention the gun. Not so far, anyway." He shook his head. "Frakes got lynched in the press, and the mayor wants to throw him to the wolves. Fucking shame, man."

I nodded. "I saw it a hundred times in homicide."

After a pause, Zucco asked me what I was doing now, and before I could answer, Verity said, "Mike's a private investigator. He's working on those Club Belgrade murders. Working for the insurance company."

Zucco smiled. "Really? Nothing personal, Mike, but—fat chance clearing that one." He shook his head and his face reddened a little, maybe thinking I'd take umbrage.

"Come on, Emil, give the guy a break," said Verity.

"No, listen, no offense, Mike. Hey, if anybody could clear that, I bet it would be somebody like yourself. But you know as well as I do, those were outfit jobs. Classic." He tipped up a long neck and drank.

I asked, "Did either of you ever hear of a place called Demon Lover, something like that?"

Verity looked at Zucco, then at me. "What kind of a place?"

"I'm not sure. Club or a bar, I guess."

Verity bunched his chin, shook his head, then shifting his eyes to Zucco, said, "Ask the vice guy."

Zucco was shaking his head, too, but he looked intrigued. "Sounds familiar," he said. "I just can't place it."

"Well I'm not surprised, it's not listed in the phone book, not anywhere in the Chicago area."

"Wait," he said. "I know that name for some reason." Zucco tapped his lower lip, then eyes brightening, he said, "I know! It's not a bar, it's the name of a company. It's a corporation, they own lots of clubs. There's one near Crystal Lake—Earth Angels, it's called. You know that place, Hank? Just north of town, on Route 14."

"Never heard of it," Verity said.

"It's a gentleman's club, nude dancers."

Verity laughed. "The fuck would I know about a gentleman's club?"

"Not much, since you got to be a gentleman to get in."

"And they let *you* in?"

Zucco's smile softened. "It was an investigation we had, kind of an interesting case—a little out of the ordinary for us, anyway. This company was supposed to be involved in some sort of sex slave deal, importing women here from Eastern Europe. Bosnia, places like that."

"So what happened?" I asked.

"The whole thing turned out to be unfounded."

"Bullshit, unfounded," Verity spat. His reaction came so abruptly, seemed so out of place, that Zucco and I just stared at him. Verity shifted his eyes a little self-consciously then, and said, "I mean, I know for a fact that stuff really happens, and it's a fucking shame no one does anything about it." His eyes grew dark and he scanned the room idly, and in his silence he seemed to have left us. I was beginning to see that Verity really was an odd duck.

Zucco took a stab at levity, "Hank came on this job to save the world. Can you believe this guy? He still thinks it's all on the square."

Verity snickered good-naturedly, but didn't say anything, and the silence was getting uncomfortable. Finally, I took a risk and said, "Hank, it does have the earmarks of an urban legend, though, doesn't it? Kind of like alligators in the New York sewers? I mean I just don't get how you could bring women halfway around the world against their will. How would you even get them in the country? And once they're here, how do you keep them from just walking away?"

"I know, that's the thing, Hank," Zucco said.

"They bring them to Mexico first, then across the border," Verity said, as though it was an established fact.

"Well, I can tell you, buddy," Zucco said, "the whole thing turned out to be unfounded."

"Unfounded, bullshit," Verity said. "What you mean is, you couldn't prove it. But it happens."

"We talked to lots of those girls, Henry, and none of them had any complaints."

"And what did you think they're gonna say?"

"Fine," Zucco said. "And how do you prove a crime without a victim?"

"That's not the point, Emil. It's that word, 'unfounded.' When we can't prove something, we just call it 'unfounded.' Like if we can't find it, it didn't happen—and that's just plain bullshit."

"Like WMDs in Iraq," I said.

Both men looked at me, their eyes asking me what the hell

my point was, then Verity said, "Urban legend, my ass." He pecked the air with his finger for emphasis. "I'm telling you, Mike, I know that shit happens. It's going on right now."

"Hey, don't get mad, Hank," I said, trying a friendly laugh. "We're just having a conversation."

Zucco laughed, too. "Yeah, Hank, what the hell's the matter with you?"

Verity raised both palms. "Sorry. This stuff just really gets me steaming. I know it happens, Mike, and they're getting away with it because there just doesn't seem to be any way to stop them, not legally. They get these women to come here on some pretext, tell them there's these great jobs waiting for them in America, secretarial jobs, modeling jobs, like that. No experience necessary. These girls are so poor it would make you sick, and they fall for it. So these parasites smuggle them in, and the girls got no papers, and they're forced into brothels, or forced to strip in these clubs. There's no place they can go, and if they even think about trying to get away, these goons beat the piss out of them."

Looking at me, Zucco wagged his head toward Verity. "Guy thinks he's gonna save the world." Then to Verity he said, "You know, that makes a great story, Hank. So where's your proof?"

"Just because you can't prove it doesn't mean it's not true."

"Hank," I asked, "are you talking about this Demon Lover organization?"

"Well—I can't say I heard of that organization, no. I just know it happens."

"How?" Zucco was challenging him now. "How do you know, Hank?"

"Street sources."

"Right," Zucco chuckled. "Confidential sources."

"Yeah." He met Zucco's eyes and didn't smile.

"Reliable informants," Zucco smirked.

"Whatever," Verity said, looking away now, reconsidering his stance. "It happens. Let's talk about something else."

They started talking about soccer—kid's soccer. Henry happened to coach Zucco's kid in the Edison Park league. I excused myself.

CHAPTER THIRTEEN

I headed for the bar, really wanting something with a little more heft than beer, but the crowd had grown even deeper, so I left. Walking the two blocks to my car, it occurred to me that I could drive out to Earth Angels, the place Zucco had mentioned near Crystal Lake, scope the place out and get a drink there. And then pulling away, I remembered that Earth Angels wasn't far from Sutler's Grove, where Beth lived. I could pick up Stapler at my apartment and drop him off. Delighted by the prospect of seeing Beth, I called her on my cell phone and told her I was headed up her way. "How about I drop Stapler off tonight?"

There was a short silence. "Well—I'm going out. What time would you come?"

"I could be there by eight-thirty."

Another hesitation. "Okay, Mike. But someone's picking me up at nine, if you can be here before then?"

"I'll be there by eight-thirty."

"But are you sure? I mean, it's a long way to come, and well—I won't have time to visit or anything."

I told her it was no problem, then turned in the direction of my apartment, dialing directory assistance for the number of Earth Angels. A recorded message said they were open until three a.m., four on weekends, closed on Sunday.

Headed north on I-90 toward Sutler's Grove, Stapler keeping an eye on traffic from the copilot's position, Beth's words replayed in my head. She was going out, but not until later—"someone" was picking her up. So where does an unattached woman go at nine at night, and with whom? I had a picture of a youthful Bohemian, some shaggy artist who would whisper in her ear about painting as he slipped off her panties. I used to think of Beth as an archetype: the nice, Catholic girl. She really had been a virgin when I married her, and even going through the divorce, she once remarked that in the eyes of God, we would always be married. Much later, I brought that up to her, in truth rather clumsily, and she laughed at me and said, "I didn't say I would remain a *celibate,* for God's sake!"

I dropped coins in the basket at the Elgin toll plaza, then pulling away I wished I had put this off, had come on an evening when I could spend a little time with her. That may have been the reason she tried to discourage me from coming tonight. It gave me a small thrill: what if she actually *wanted* to spend a little time with me?

And what if tonight I just told her flat out, *I'm still in love with you. Give us another chance, Beth. I promise, I promise—you won't be sorry. We can take it slow, get reacquainted.* Maybe if I said those things, she wouldn't even go out tonight. Maybe she'd cancel her date with whoever, and stay home with me.

Why not just do it! Do it now, tonight! But I sat back, already knowing the answer, though it still hit me in the face like a pail of ice water: a) You don't have the guts to say it; b) you couldn't promise her you'd remain faithful, not even at your age; and c) what would you have left if she shot you down?

At eight-fifteen I parked under the street lamp in front of Beth's big Victorian, its tall windows dropping yellow rectangles of light onto the lawn. I put Stapler on a leash and walked him to the front door, the light from the street lamp sprinkling odd shapes through the big willow tree onto the gingerbread exterior.

On the porch I twisted the little key on the door and jangled a bell.

Beth was even prettier than the picture of her I keep in my head, standing there backlit in the doorway, beaming that delightful smile, and for a moment I had the fantasy that she'd groomed herself just for me. But she was going out. "Someone" would be here soon.

Before she spoke to me she knelt, rubbed Stapler's ears. He licked her face. "Oh, you are such a pretty boy," she said.

"Thank you," I said. She stood, her smiling eyes coming in to mine. "Oh, you meant him?"

She chuckled.

"Yup," I said, "Stapler brought Mikey along."

She laughed and kissed my cheek. "Mike, I wish I could invite you in, but—" She opened her hands in a gesture of helplessness. "You know I'm going out, right?"

The spot on my check where she kissed me pulsed warmly. I said, "No problem, I understand," and handed her the leash. Stapler—the rat—stepped inside and around her legs without even a look back. Beth had to switch hands as he sniffed the air.

"How about I give you a call tomorrow?" she said.

"Fine," I said. The warm spot seemed to glow, connecting electrically to my groin.

"Thanks so much, Mike. I really mean it." She fluttered her fingertips at me said, "Bye, now," and shut the door.

I walked back to my car, and for a fleeting moment thought of parking in the shadows down the block to get a look at whoever showed up at her door. And to see how she acted with him. It wasn't an urge borne of some sordid trait, not necessarily. After all, spying on people is a big part of my business. But I wanted to think I'd grown up a little since Beth and I parted, that I'd developed a little respect for her space, her privacy. And I'd grown up enough, too, to anticipate the pain that was bound to come, seeing her with another man.

I crossed the old railroad tracks out of Sutler's Grove and followed back roads until I intersected Route 14, then turned toward Crystal Lake looking for Earth Angels, not sure exactly where along the highway it was. But it wasn't hard to find, its lights blossoming out of the darkness, a low-slung structure with a huge sign in pink neon blinking "Totally Nude! Totally Nude! Totally Nude!" That must have made for some interesting effects on the walls of the run-down apartments across the way.

The parking area was lit up like a used car lot, the cars filling it in the reverse manner of Sunday morning church services. The rows close to the front door were filled, but the back row along Route 14 nearly empty. I found a spot in the last pew. I should have guessed that no one particularly wanted his car seen from the road. Later, I'd regret not having figured that out.

Inside, it wasn't the twenty-dollar price of admission that shocked me, nor was it the rule that you had to buy at least one drink. It wasn't even the admonition, in big, bold letters:

"You cannot touch the girls. You cannot proposition the girls."

What bothered me was what the guy with the Popeye arms at the cash register told me: "We don't serve alcohol."

"You mean I can't get a drink?"

He looked at me as if I were a slow child. "No, you can get about any kind of a drink you want, so long as it don't have alcohol in it."

A girl standing next to him, about twenty in an ivory tunic that Diana the Huntress would have worn, gave me a wicked smile and said, "Don't worry, sweety, I'll intoxicate you." The dress material must have been expensive; she wasn't wearing much of it.

I smiled back and went in, the light subdued, a stage with a pole spotlighted in the far corner. A couple of guys in their early twenties were sitting at the edge of the stage wearing backward baseball caps, but most of the customers hunkered over small black tables the size of LP records scattered throughout the room. I made my way to a table in the back, edging past an enormously fat guy sitting alone on the padded bench that ran the length of the wall. A waitress dressed like Tarzan's Jane came over, and I ordered a Coke.

The music started, heavy on the bass, an announcer beseeching the small audience to "Give it up for Crystal!" and a leggy, platinum blonde in black negligee and sword-length heels slinked onto the stage. Crystal danced and stripped and swung on the pole, then with sultry eyes she got completely naked except for the heels and a garter, and lay on her back and writhed. Then a bald guy sitting at the edge of the stage reached toward her with a bill, and she scooted her butt along the stage to get closer and he stuck it in her garter. Grinning, she got to her knees, took him by the ears and kissed the top of his head. "Thanks, Hon," she said. Then she put her sultry expression back on and started writhing again, but the spell was broken for me.

From the corner of my eye I spotted the girl in the Diana costume in the doorway scanning the room, and when her eye fell on me, she sauntered over. She knelt up on the seat next to me and told me her name was Bambi. "Would you like a lap dance?" Leaning near me, she tugged down the top of her dress to give her breasts a little more air than they needed, maybe exposing a nipple or two. It was pretty dark.

"Thanks," I said, "but I think I'll just watch the show."

"You sure? It only costs twenty bucks. What's your name, sweetie?"

"Homer," I said.

"Homer," she cooed, "I can put my pussy this close to your face." Indicating a very small opening between her thumb and forefinger.

I suppose for some guys that prospect is a turn-on, but as much as I have a weakness for beautiful women—and she was beautiful—I tend to be attracted to the sum of all their parts. The gestalt, if you will. And the idea of Bambi's naked crotch pumping away an inch from my face, not to mention my nose, was a lesson in anatomy I did not crave.

"No thanks, Bambi."

"You don't think I'm pretty?" she pouted.

"You're beautiful," I said.

"What's the matter then, can't afford twenty bucks?"

I guess that was meant to shame me. I'd have happily paid twenty bucks to talk to one of these dancers for the length of time it took to do a lap dance, but I was looking for immigrant women, and Bambi was as American as bubble gum, and an airhead to boot. Maybe it was part of the act—her name was Bambi like mine was Homer—but I doubted I could get her to break character long enough to tell me anything useful, and it just wasn't worth the risk of drawing attention to myself.

"Right, Bambi. I'm afraid I just can't afford it."

"Okay, Homer," she said, and walked away looking miffed. But she didn't go far. She knelt on the cushioned bench next to the fat guy, and a minute later she was moving to the beat, her body writhing near his, letting her hair fall around his face, now slipping out of her dress, plunging her breasts close to his cheek, now slipping off her panties, standing astraddle him on the cushion, her crotch inches from his face, driving in time to the music. He sat there like a stone Buddha. And a feminist will tell you that this whole business is degrading to *women.*

Neither Bambi nor Crystal were foreigners, and I'd had about enough of this, was getting up to leave when Opal came on stage. There was something in the Slavic planes of her face that told me she wasn't born here, and I changed my mind. Opal was a little more athletic. She leaped, planted her heels around the pole and hung upside down.

Her number finished, Opal left the stage and a short time later was working the tables. She stopped to talk to the two kids in baseball caps, and I thought she was going to do a lap dance there, but she took one of them by the hand and led him off through a door. I sat watching Absinthe, the dancer of the moment.

When she left the stage I noticed the kid whom Opal had led into the back had returned to his table, and two minutes after that Opal materialized through the same door, paused there a minute, then headed straight across the room toward me.

"Would you like a dance?" Her eyes were dark, her voice steamier than Bambi's, the accent European—Serbian, I thought, the same as I'd heard at Club Belgrade. I wanted to make some connection with her, but was it worth going through that?

"I'm sorry," she said with a captivating smile. "The music is so loud. I said, would you like a dance?"

"No, thank you. But I liked your dance up there." I was beginning to wonder if there was something wrong with me. Watching this stuff was actually lowering my libido. Every grain of enchanting feminine mystery had fled this room.

"That's very sweet of you," she said, and walked away. Her smile seemed genuine, and I wished there would have been some way to talk to her. But I let it go.

The place filled with patrons as the evening wore on, and I watched every dancer until closing time. They would perform for about ten minutes, men hovering at the edge of the stage, thrusting bills into their garters, then the dance ended they'd leave the stage and reappear among the patrons and move from table to table, stopping now and then to perform a lap dance. A few more dancers asked if I wanted a dance, and when I declined they moved on to flirt with other customers. Some had European accents, but none betrayed the slightest displeasure with her calling—they seemed to genuinely enjoy their work, the European girls as much as the others.

I pulled from the parking lot and on an impulse crossed Route 14 into the apartment complex, parked facing the club, and cut my lights. After nearly an hour, the flashing sign winked off and all the exterior lights went dark, the remaining customers straggling out to their cars and driving off. About ten minutes after the last customer was gone, a group of three girls and a guy came out. One of the girls—I thought it was Bambi—yelled something I couldn't understand as she walked to her car, and the other two girls laughed. The guy watched them drive off and went back inside. Less than five minutes later he came out again, this time with five girls. These he escorted to a big van parked in a shadow at the back of the lot. He slid the back door open, the girls climbed in, he got into the driver's seat and they pulled off.

When the van passed under a streetlight I got a better look at it: maroon Dodge Ram, older model in need of some bodywork. I didn't get the plate number, and watched it turn onto Route 14.

I followed, staying a couple of blocks behind. In Crystal Lake it turned, followed a complicated route which brought it to I-90, and descended the ramp headed south. It took the Route 53 north exit, then turned onto Algonquin Road and followed it into Mount Prospect, where it turned again and snaked its way through a maze of back streets, and stopped on a street lined with three-flats. I parked about half a block back and watched the girls file into the building. I thought the driver went in, too, which was a mistake. I gave it a minute, then pulled up behind the van and jotted down the license number. Then I saw the driver was still sitting behind the wheel. I pulled out, and he turned and looked at me as I drove past. I wasn't sure how good a look he got, but I got a real good look at him. It was Tony, the bouncer at Club Belgrade.

CHAPTER FOURTEEN

Out of the house early the following morning, I drove over to the Albany Park police station to talk to Officer Smoot, the one whose beat covered Club Belgrade, the one who'd arrested me that night. I was hoping to catch him as he was going off duty.

Traffic was already thickening, and in the slow pace I reflected on the Club Belgrade/Demon Lover connection. Was there one? Eva said Tony worked for Demon Lover. Maybe it really was just a different job, like Eva had suggested. Or tried to suggest. Her body language that night seemed to betray something more.

I reached the station before seven and parked across the street where I could keep an eye on the cars pulling into the lot. Smoot arrived about seven-fifteen, nosing his squad car into a spot against the station wall. He arranged some things on the seat next to him, then sat staring at the bricks, waiting for his relief.

I walked over. He rolled down the window, his eyes full of that patient resolve you might show an insurance salesman.

"I just got a couple of questions, Smoot," I said.

"I'm busy."

"You're not going anywhere until your relief comes out. It'll just take a minute."

"You don't pick up on hints real good, do you? So how about this? Fuck off."

I leaned closer. "Listen up, shithead. I had a nice talk with Wolfgang Bauer, and with his boss, Stepan Vasil. I know all about your monthly at Club Belgrade. Now sooner or later what I uncover is going to hit the papers, and that little bit of information could make an investigative reporter cream her panties."

His lips came open, blood rising to his face. Then he looked away, thought a minute, and when his eyes rejoined mine he hissed, "You cocksucker. I went to bat for you!"

"I don't want to hurt you, Smoot. Just don't fuck with me, okay? All I want to know is this: why weren't you there the morning Krunic got it?"

He looked to the wall again. Then without looking at me, he said, "I was on my way to the club. I was about three blocks away and I got a call to come into the station. I went in. That's where I was when the call came in about Krunic."

So. Since Smoot's car was down, they assigned the job to another car. Pretty simple—that happened more often than not, so what the hell did I expect? I felt a little sheepish, but at least I'd laid some boundaries with Smoot. I didn't want to make him an enemy, but better that than let him take me for a patsy. "Okay," I said. "Then what was the big deal? Why didn't you just tell me that in the first place?" He didn't answer. I turned to go.

"Duncavan?" he said.

I turned to look at him.

"Why don't you go fuck yourself?"

Which made me think of one more question. "Smoot, you didn't say what they called you into the station for."

His eyes locked on mine and his jaw slid forward, wanting to play his little power game. "I, don't, know," he said, punctuating the words, his eye steady on mine for a five-count. Then he laid his wrist on the steering wheel and turned away. "The dispatcher told me to go in and see the watch commander. When I got there, the watch commander was on the phone. I waited, and when he got off the phone he said he didn't call me in. He said to check with the desk. I did, but no one knew anything about it. So I just went back on the street."

"And you went straight to the scene then?"

"Yeah," he said, still looking away, his jaw working. "I went over there, but another car had the job."

"Smoot?" I said.

His eyes smoldered into mine.

"It wasn't your fault, man," I said, and patted his shoulder. He didn't move.

I drove to the office, the inbound Kennedy at a bumper-to-bumper crawl, feeling badly for Smoot. I had no doubt he was a good copper, though he'd surely be fired if it came out that he was taking money to see Krunic safely to his car. And it was probably eating his gut raw that Krunic got killed anyway, and there was probably no one he could talk to about it. Coppers aren't big on talking out their feelings. Something you had to admire them for.

Although his summons to the station came just minutes before Krunic was murdered, it was probably a coincidence—at least there was no reason to think otherwise. The dispatcher could have gotten the car number wrong. Or whoever called the communications center could have given it wrong. Maybe the message was delayed, and by the time Smoot got the message, whoever wanted him had gone home. Or maybe the guy who called was in the john. There could be a thousand explanations—who knew? And what difference did it make? I filed it away under "Miscellaneous."

Chapter Fifteen

In the office a couple of days later, I dialed Beth's number to see how she was doing with Stapler. I got her answering machine and left a message to call me. Then I called my old partner, Marty Richter, hoping he might help sort things out. When it came to stalled investigations, Marty was about the best sounding board you could find. Though even calling this one "stalled" exaggerated my progress. What progress?

I reached Marty at the station. He said he was heading down to a meeting at police headquarters later, and planned to head home afterward. We agreed to meet at Monk's Pub, about two blocks from my office, when his meeting was over.

"One more thing, long as I got you," I said. "Can you run a plate for me?"

"Sure, I'll do it right now if you can hang on a minute. What's the number?"

I gave him the plate number of the van that had transported the girls from Earth Angels the night before, and he put me on hold. When he came back he said, "Dodge Van, registered to Demon Lover, Inc., 58 W. Jackson, Suite 1457. Isn't that The Monadnock building?" The Monadnock was a Louis Sullivan landmark at the opposite end of the Loop from my office.

"I think so," I said.

I hung up, paid some bills, then noticed that the sunlight was igniting a green haze of new buds on the spindly trees across from my window. Spring was definitely unpacking her baggage—a nice day for a walk.

The Monadnock, a jewel of Chicago architecture, hunkered on the corner of Jackson and Dearborn, a burnt-umber cliff dwelling that mocked the glass and steel monstrosities which encircled it. Its interior still retained much of the integrity of the original design. I got off the elevator on the fourteenth floor, the corridor dimly lit by fixtures which I assumed duplicated the gas lights of an earlier era, and walked the length of the corridor past oak-trimmed office fronts, their big, frosted glass windows spilling extra light onto the mosaic tile, in search of 1457. I reached the wrought-iron circular staircase at the end and retraced my steps before finding it, a tiny office tucked behind a stairwell. There was no lettering on the glass. I knocked; no one answered. Light ignited the frosted glass, though it was probably sunlight through those generous exterior windows. I tried the knob: locked.

On the other side of the Loop I met Marty, who was sitting at a table waiting for me at Monk's Pub. He had already ordered a pitcher of Killian's Red and two glasses, and as he poured I started telling him about Club Belgrade, Demon Lover, and Earth Angels. I also told him Lieutenant Verity's opinion about the trafficking in women from Bosnia. Marty must have been hungry. Listening politely, he polished off the bowl of peanuts on the table, then asked the bartender to bring another one.

"You ever heard of anything like that?" I asked. "White slavery in Chicago?"

His cupped hand full of peanuts rested on his belly. "I missed lunch, the meeting ran overtime," he said. He picked out a peanut, examined it. "Sure, I've heard of it. Have you ever heard that Proctor & Gamble is run by a Satanic cult? That's their secret symbol on the box, the man in the moon inside the circle of stars." He popped the peanut in his mouth.

"Come on, Marty. Lieutenant Verity believes it."

"Verity's a putz." He popped another peanut.

"You know Verity?"

Marty chewed, nodded his head. "Yeah, I got to know him pretty good, we made lieutenant at the same time. We went through the class together."

"Seems like a straight shooter to me."

Marty took a swig of Killian's, sat back. "You're right, I shouldn't knock the guy. He is a good egg, he's just in the wrong profession. Did you know he was almost a priest?"

"Yeah? What's almost?"

"About as close as you could get. He was ordained a deacon at Mundelein. Then just before he was supposed to take holy orders he backed out. Now he thinks he's on the street to minister to people. I'm serious. That's not good, Mike."

"The guys who work for him speak pretty well of him."

"Yeah, and the whores love him, too. You know why? He treats them all like they're Mary Magdaline." He paused. "Verity does stand up for his men, though, I'll say that for him. But if he wasn't gonna be a priest, he should have been a social worker."

Marty lit a cigarette. "Listen, you won't believe this. The guy actually puts his men through encounter sessions. I'm not shittin' you, *encounter sessions.* If there's some friction in the unit, personality clashes, stuff like that, he shuts the guys up in a room and makes them talk it out. He tells them they have to be honest about their feelings. *Feelings,* for Christ sake—this is a copper talking! You see what I mean, though? Guy's got a loose screw somewhere."

"He's a very bright guy, though," I said. "And he really believes this sex slavery business is a fact."

"I know, but listen, this thing is always popping up, a rumor. Nobody but Verity believes this white slavery bullshit, except maybe people who talk to themselves on the bus. This is America. The broads could just walk away any time they wanted to." He turned his face away, blew out a stream of smoke. "And anyway, what does any of that have to do with the murder case you're working on?"

I thought he was challenging me. "No idea," I said. "It's too early in the game."

He leaned on his forearms. "You're right, not fair. Okay, so you got any hunches? I still lay odds it's a mob hit. Or at least it's someone inside the organization. Whatsizname, the surviving partner? He's got all the money, plus the whole operation to himself now, doesn't he? Pretty convenient."

"I was beginning to get the idea that the club business maybe wasn't worth having," I said. "But now, if there's a connection—" I stopped myself from saying "white slavery connection" "—I mean, the enterprise could be bigger than it looks."

"Which means it's all about control of the enterprise. It's a classic hit. Especially if you're talking broads and strip joints."

"I don't know. That's all legal."

"Yeah, but prostitution isn't legal. Where you've got broads getting naked and dancing in guys' laps, they're not far from walking the guy to a back room where the real money is. Real quick money. I think it's pretty obvious. What you've got here are two ageless stories: the world's oldest profession meets Cain and Abel. If these guys weren't knocked off by their partner, it was someone who wants in on the action. Or else wants to eliminate the competition." He waited for me to respond. When I didn't, he shook his head and smiled. "I hate to bust your bubble, Mike. No, really, but I know you want me to be straight with you. It all adds up to a couple of mob hits—I use the term loosely. Not the Dago mafia, maybe it's a Serbian mafia. Any way you look at it, though, these are two murders with no witnesses and no one talking, and they ain't never going to be cleared."

"Well, just hang on a minute. If that's the case, why two ritual killings?"

"The first one," Marty was shaking his head, "I don't know if I'd call it 'ritual.' "

"I would. What the hell, why not just blow the guy away, like any run-of-the-mill hit? Why the bag over the head? It was suf-focation—the plastic bag—that killed him, not the ligatures around the neck."

Marty was not moved. He lifted his shoulders, eyebrows, and palms all at once. "Who the fuck knows? But hey, I guess there's a bright side. You're getting paid by the hour, and you can work on this one 'til doomsday. I hate insurance companies, I hope you milk the fuckers dry."

"Tell me something," I said, changing course. "Smoot got a call to come into the station that morning, just minutes before Krunic got it. There's computers in the cars now, something we didn't have when I was working the street. So would that mes-sage go through the dispatcher, or to the computer?"

"Could be either. You can send a message directly to the car's computer from the station if you want, tell the car to come in. You can also send a computer message to the communications center, ask the dispatcher to call the car in. Or you can pick up the phone and call the dispatcher."

"So the simplest way would be to contact the car directly?"

Marty grinned. "Why do you care about this?"

"Just like to keep up on procedures."

"Well, as a matter of fact, I'd rather type a message to the dispatcher, have him tell the car to come in."

"Why not just go direct to the car?"

"Because that way, his sergeant and all the other cars hear the call and they all know the guy's status." He took a slug of beer, set it down. "And I like to leave a paper trail whenever I can—there's a record. But if you think this means anything—" He shook his head.

"I don't. But listen, what I'm about to tell you is confidential. I found out that Club Belgrade was Smoot's monthly, and—"

Marty interrupted. "The beat guy had a monthly? I thought they quit that stuff a long time ago."

"Marty, this is confidential."

"Right, like I really give a crap. The guy's taking a hell of a risk, though. If he's caught, he'll blow this job. These patrol officers, they're making good dough now."

"Anyway, it just seems a strange coincidence that he gets called away minutes before the murder."

Marty smirked. "Okay," he said. "So you think the watch commander did it?"

That pushed my hot button. "Listen, *you* could have done it. So quit FUCKING with me." It came out louder than I intended. The couple at the next table looked over.

"Mike, Mike, Mike," Marty said. "You bring a tear to my eye, you know that? My old partner, coming back."

CHAPTER SIXTEEN

That night I sat in my living room thinking about what Marty had told me about Lieutenant Verity having been in the seminary. It explained a lot about the way he'd been talking at Frakes's fund-raiser, about Frakes being "compassionate." And it explained, maybe, his odd reaction to the subject of sex slaves. So Verity was a crusader. Did that mean I might be able to enlist him as an ally? He had no reason to trust me, let alone help me.

Then I thought of Bill Spina, a lawyer and close friend who actually had been a priest, had done parish work for a few years before giving it up. Bill was older than Verity, but he still might know him. And anyway, I really didn't know how old Verity was, except that he was older than he looked.

Bill Spina had defended me back when I tanked my legal career, stood by me at a time when a lot of people at the bar of justice turned their backs. My misdeed was not a small one: in the middle of a trial, in a fever of hot blood, I punched out my opposing counsel, then when the deputy tried to stop me, I decked him, too. Now comes the really hard part. As the judge tried to escape the courtroom, I nailed him right behind the court reporter's chair. She never missed a beat, either, which didn't help my case—it was all on the record. I still cringe, thinking about it.

Spina, who shortly before that ugly incident had left the State Attorney's office, called me and volunteered his services. He kept me out of jail—in itself no small miracle—and worked out a plea bargain: Court supervision in exchange for voluntary surrender of my law license and one hundred sixty hours' community service. For a few weeks, I joined a gang of orange-vested prodigals who, under the supervision of a deputy sheriff, picked up trash along the roadsides. When my period of supervision ended, Bill got my conviction record expunged—otherwise, I could never have gotten a private investigator's license. And Bill would not accept a dime.

I called Spina when I reached my office. His secretary said he was in Los Angeles on a deposition, that he'd be back in a couple of days. I didn't leave a message.

That afternoon I drove out to Mount Prospect for a daylight look at the apartment building where Tony dropped off the van-load of women. It was a garden-variety three flat in a neighborhood of similar buildings. I parked and went up the walk, wanting to get a look at the names on the mailboxes, but the vestibule door was locked.

I sat in my car for a couple of hours, working crossword puzzles and watching the front door. A few people came and went, none looking like an exotic dancer. With all that time to think, I had a creeping sense that a dead end for this investigation was just around the next curve. So I resolved to do that which I hate most: an extended stake out.

The following week I spent the afternoon hours sitting in a rental car, a different one each day, listening to books on tape and watching the building. Twice during that week I'd left messages on Beth's answering machine, but she didn't call back. I had plenty of time, sitting there for all those hours, to worry about why she didn't call, imagining the worst.

Every day about five in the afternoon, the maroon van would park in front. The girls would file out of the building, climb in and be whisked off, usually by Tony, sometimes by a Mexican guy I never saw before. But if the girls were prisoners, they sure didn't act like it. Sometimes they laughed and joked, sometimes making fun of Tony, who seemed to have no sense of humor. He would just stand there stony-faced, his hand on the van's door handle, then slide it shut when they were all aboard.

I graduated from books on tape to old-time radio shows, Jack Benny and Charlie McCarthy and *Gunsmoke*, each day growing longer than the day before. Why wouldn't Beth return my calls?

In my daily observance I began to detect different personalities among the girls filing out of the building; one kind of shy, one a jokester, one very serious. The only one whose name I knew was Opal. But except for their daily van routine, rarely would any of them come or go. Once in a while one would leave during the day, but always in the company of a man. They didn't act like prisoners, but their movement did seem restricted.

Then one day I was driving to the building, one of those April afternoons that convertible owners yearn for, sunny and warm and filled with the promise of summer, and saw something truly bizarre. I was stopped at a red light across from a Wal-Mart, about a mile from the apartment. On the corner across the street, a girl about eighteen years old, wearing a simple cotton dress, was kneeling on the sidewalk. A Hispanic guy was standing next to her, holding her hand, looking bored. Was she suddenly overcome with a need to pray, right there on the sidewalk? Or had the guy just chased her down and caught her?

The light changed, the car behind me honked. I tried to get into the left-turn lane to turn into the Wal-Mart lot, but couldn't. I drove on, found a driveway. By the time I got turned around and reached the corner again, the two were walking across the Wal-Mart lot. The guy was still holding her hand, leading her. She followed as though in a trance.

I turned into the lot and swung back in their direction. They were nearing a van, much like the one Tony drove, only this one was dark green.

I parked and as I walked toward them the man ushered the girl into the backseat, slid the door shut, and got in on the front passenger's side. All the van's windows were open. I saw now that the girl was sitting next to another girl behind the driver. The other one was about the same age and dress. Behind the two, an older woman, maybe sixty-five, occupied the third seat, the type you might see parked in a lawn chair in front of a trailer with a quart of beer on her knee.

"Are you okay, Miss?" I asked the girl through the open window. She kept her eyes straight ahead, her expression blank. She didn't look at me.

The guy in the front passenger seat craned his head around. "Now, who the fuck are you?"

"Miss, are you okay?" She still didn't answer.

The guy clambered out and slammed the door so hard it rocked the van. "Look, man, get the fuck out of here and mind your own business." He was about my height, swarthy complexion, maybe twenty-five. He stood with his face in mine, clenching and unclenching his fists.

"Excuse me," I said, "but I can't hear the lady." I asked her again, "Are you okay?"

Now the driver jumped out and ran around the front of the van and took a position next to his pal, the two of them with murder in their eyes. I started backing away, and just then a woman in shorts came rattling past with a loaded shopping cart. She looked over, then looked away. She stopped behind a Jeep across the aisle, popped the tail gate, and started loading her groceries.

"Get the fuck out of here, man," the first guy said, keeping his voice low.

Then the driver looked at him and said, "What're we doin'?

Why don't we just fuckin' leave, man?"

The first one considered that, then without answering he climbed back into the passenger's seat and slammed the door again. The driver walked around and climbed back in, and when he started the engine, I grabbed the door handle and slid the back door open.

"What the fuck!" the guy in the passenger seat scrambled out once more, came over and put his face inches from mine. You could almost see the steam coming off his head. The lady across the aisle stopped unloading her cart and looked at us.

Now the older woman in the rear-most seat rasped. "She's all right, Mister." Her smile was friendly, with a couple of gaps in her teeth. "She was just having some female problems. Havin' some cramps is all, and she needed to get some air." Ay-er, she said.

"Is that right, Miss?" I asked.

Instead of answering, the girl raised a hand to shield her face from me.

The woman in back spoke again. "She don't speak American. But she's fine." Fahn. The woman reached up and stroked the girl's hair. "You're fine, now, aren't ya, hon?" The girl turned to face me for the first time.

"Yes, yes," she said in a foreign accent, blinking back tears, her eyes clinging to mine.

The guy shot his arm in front of me to the door handle and slammed it shut, then climbed into the front passenger's seat. "Let's go," he said, and banged his fist on the dashboard. The driver backed out, and as he turned toward the exit I took down the license number, then went to my car as quickly as I could. I tried to follow, but by the time I pulled from my parking spot they'd already made a right turn onto Algonquin Road—the opposite direction from the apartment. The lady in the Jeep pulled out ahead of me, rolling slowly toward the exit, taking her sweet time. By the time I reached the street, the van was nowhere in sight. I followed in that direction for a while, but never spotted it again.

CHAPTER SEVENTEEN

I ran a check on the van's plate from my office the following morning. It was registered to Demon Lover, Inc. Then I sat at my office window, a sudden April shower hurling itself against the pane, umbrellas sprouting up and down the sidewalk, traffic on Washington compressing and stretching itself like some oily cosmic worm. It looked as though Lieutenant Henry Verity's instincts could be right on the money. There was something bad going on.

And I had to face it: if I had what I thought I had, I was way over my head. I couldn't go this alone, not without some co-operation from the cops.

I picked up the phone then, called Area Five Violent Crimes and asked for Wally Phelps, not really knowing what I would say to him.

Detective Dalton answered. Dalton, I remembered, was one of the team assigned to the Krunic murder. I asked for Phelps.

"Phelps has been transferred to the training division," he said. He did not sound friendly.

I hesitated, hoping I'd heard wrong. "He's *detailed* to the training division?" I asked hopefully. That would mean he was assigned to the academy temporarily—for training, something like that.

"Who is this?" Dalton was not in the mood to answer questions.

"I'm an old friend, Detective. I was just up at the Area to see him last week."

He warmed a little. "No, he's been transferred to the Academy as an instructor. Far as I know, it's a permanent assignment. You want the phone number there?"

I took down the number, called the academy and left a message. Wally called me back twenty minutes later. "I've been waiting for this assignment forever, Mike," he said. "Actually I'd given up on it, and then all of a sudden the order came out of the blue. It's great, working hours like a regular human being, Saturdays and Sundays off. I'm teaching Criminal Investigations—stop by some day, Mike. The Academy is really something to see, now, compared to that old tomb we went through on O'Brien Street. We'll have lunch, okay?" His tone signaled the end of the conversation.

"Wally," I said.

"What?"

"This investigation—I need to, ah, coordinate with the police somehow. The team that's handling it, Dalton and O'Toole—are they approachable?"

"They're kind of—" He went silent for a full six seconds. "No, Mike. I already talked to them about you. They were pretty cool to the idea of—of getting involved with you. They do know I showed you the file, though. I mean, they okayed that."

I said goodbye. I guess I understood. If Dalton and O'Toole were treating the Club Belgrade murders as back-burner cases, they didn't need me around, maybe drawing attention to what little they had accomplished, maybe making it look like they'd dropped the ball. They had nothing to gain by cooperating with me.

So where did I go from here?

Sunlight broke against the red brick façade across from my window, even as rain still dropped on umbrellas below. And suddenly I thought of Henry Verity—could I make him an ally?

At this point I had nothing to lose by trying. But how to approach him? How would he react? He had no reason to cooperate with me, either.

I decided to try calling Bill Spina again. An ex-priest himself, he seemed to know just about everybody who'd spent time in the seminary. This time, I reached him at his office.

"Hey, Mike, where you been hiding?" he said.

"You got a minute?"

"Sorry, I'm out the door on my way to court. Can you meet me for lunch?" Before I could answer, he said, "Illinois Athletic Club, eleven-thirty. Come on, it'll be great to see you."

"I want to buy *you* lunch," I said.

"Don't worry, I'll bill it to some file." He chuckled. I knew his ethics, knew it was a joke. "Eleven-thirty, Mike."

We sat at a table overlooking Grant Park, the green grass like a giant pool table in the sunlight. I was actually craving a cocktail, but Bill ordered a Pepsi, so I did, too, and watching him perusing the menu, this old friend who'd saved my life, I felt suddenly sheepish, coming to him for one more favor. I owed him so much already.

For a religious guy, Bill looked a lot like Mephistopheles: eyebrows wild and black and almost meeting above his dagger nose, a pointed beard, eyes that pierced, and a smile you could call ferocious. He wore a rumpled suit with an expensive tie, his beard grayer now, his features more chiseled than ever.

After some small talk he asked, "How can I help you, my friend?"

I gave Bill a rough sketch of the case without a lot of details. I told him it would be nice to enlist the help of a police officer in the district where it happened, then I told him about Lieutenant Henry Verity, that I'd heard he'd been in the seminary. "I thought you might know him. I heard that he went all the way to deacon, then dropped out before taking holy orders."

"Not true," he said.

"You know him?"

"Sure I know Hank. I mean it's not true he dropped out. Hank was a few classes behind me, up at the big house." A reference to Saint Mary of the Lake Seminary. "He was ordained, what? Four years after I was. He was assigned to St. Matthews, in Arlington Heights." He paused. "Actually, Hank and I got to be pretty good friends. I guess you could say I was a kind of mentor to him. Hank wasn't good at languages. You know that philosophy and theology classes were taught in Latin?"

"I'd heard that, somewhere."

"Anyway, I helped him with his Latin. Good guy, Hank."

"He was actually a priest? And he became a copper?" I couldn't hide my surprise.

He shrugged. "Listen, most of the guys from my class left. And there's not a whole lot you can do in the real world with a doctorate in sacred theology. So they did all kinds of things. Some guys went to work at city hall, some guys even went into the trades. We got a great education up there, but not terribly useful. Hank was always a kind of a crusader rabbit, anyway. Police work—I can see it."

"Why'd he leave, do you know?"

He shrugged again. "Everybody has different reasons for leaving," he said, his eyes roving the room. "Most guys eventually had a problem with celibacy. Hank, he—" His eyes came back to mine. "This is not for publication, although I guess it's no secret. Hank had a problem, a young widow in the parish. Her husband was killed in a water skiing accident—young guy, under thirty. Age-old story, she turns to her parish priest for comfort. I don't know exactly what happened, but I do know that some people thought he was giving her a little too much comfort. It turned into a minor scandal in the parish."

"So he left?"

"Uh-uh. He got transferred to another parish. But she followed him to the new parish—or so the story goes. Anyway, eventually he did leave, and he married her. I know that part's true. They're still married, far as I know."

"Have you seen him recently?"

"Sort of. We keep in contact."

"Seems odd, the story going around about him quitting before ordination. I mean, the truth makes an even better story."

Bill took a bite of a breadstick and shook his head. "Mhm-mhm. Hank probably started that story himself. Hard to hide where you went to school, and anyway Hank's very conscientious, wouldn't want to tell a lie. If he said he was ordained a deacon, that was true, since they make you a deacon first, before you take the final vows. So he could just leave it at that."

"Seems to me 'former priest' might look nice on your resume, though."

"Not true, Mike, not at all. You leave, you don't want that following you. You want to fit in. You become a ditchdigger, you don't want to be Father Ditchdigger."

"Bill, Verity might be a lot of help to me on this case. Can I use your name?"

"Sure you can use my name. You want me to give him a call?"

"You really know him that well?"

"Hank? Listen, the guy owes me."

I thought: with the generosity of this man, legions must owe him.

"Well, *I* owe you," I said. "Sure, call him."

We parted on the sidewalk on Michigan Avenue, Bill saying he'd try to reach Verity as soon as he got back to the office.

Since Verity was working midnights and probably slept afternoons, I had planned to call him myself that evening. But he called me about four o'clock that afternoon.

"Mike, Bill Spina said you wanted to talk."

"It's about that subject we talked about at Frakes's fund-raiser."

"I'm not sure what you mean."

I told him then about Earth Angels, about watching the van shepherding the girls from the apartment to the club and back. I told him the girls never went out unescorted. Then I told him about the girl kneeling on the sidewalk. When I finished, he was silent for so long I thought we'd been disconnected.

"Hello?" I said.

"I'm here. I told you there was something to all this, didn't I? But nobody wants to believe it."

Until now, I'd been struck by occasional doubts whether all this really proved anything, and suddenly I felt vindicated. "So where do we go from here?" I said, instantly regretting the presumptuous "we."

"I'll help you in any way I can, but you've got to remember, it's not my case. Vice is not my assignment. I'm a tactical lieutenant in the sixteenth district, and I have no jurisdiction in Schaumburg."

"Club Belgrade is in your district. Krunic was murdered in your district."

He was silent again. I waited. Finally, he said, "I'm not sure what that has to do with white slavery in the suburbs."

I reminded him that Tony, the driver of the van, worked at Club Belgrade, and thinking about it, I suddenly felt foolish.

"That's pretty—tenuous," he said. "Besides, aren't you confusing the issue? What happened in my district was a murder. You are talking about white slavery."

I really didn't have anything to say to that, but before I could respond he said, "Look, I'm not putting you off, I'd be pleased to help you, but—check in with me now and again, let me know how you're doing. You've got more legitimacy poking around in this than I have. At least somebody's hired you to investigate these murders. I don't work Violent Crimes."

"What about the evidence of white slavery?" I said. "I'm wondering if someone, the FBI maybe, should be alerted to that." And maybe you, Hank, should be the one to do it, was my point.

"I know," he said. "But it's just not enough. If you want to be treated like some kook who says he's been probed by space aliens, go ahead and call them. I'm not about to, not at this point, especially after what Zucco said. They've gone down this road before."

"Okay, but one more thing. There was the body of a woman found about a week ago in a forest preserve near Barrington. Unidentified. She had a plastic bag tied over her head, just like Simunic."

"I saw that on the news."

"Can you find out if homicide is doing anything with that?"

"Violent Crimes?" he corrected. "No problem. And listen, I'm not blowing you off. Let me give you my home address and phone number." He gave me an address on Osceola in Edison Park, a neighborhood nudging the northwest suburbs, filled with cops and firemen and city employees who wished they could escape the city.

Before leaving the office that afternoon, I phoned Beth again. Again I got her answering machine. I was starting to worry. If she didn't call me back the next day, I'd drive out to Sutler's Grove.

"Beth," I said to the answering machine, "I don't know what's wrong, but I do miss—" *Miss you?* I found myself so wanting to say it "—miss my dog. At least call me, all right? Let me know he's okay."

CHAPTER EIGHTEEN

I returned to Earth Angels that night, sat at the same table in the corner not far from the stage, and after a while, Opal came on. She was more exotic than the other dancers, her gauze-draped body writhing in a primordial rhythm that resurrected Eve and Helen and Salome. Then she got naked and climbed the pole, and somehow the allure was cast off with the last veil. What was wrong with me? I was a card-carrying dirty old man. I lurked in my office window and mentally undressed the lovelies passing below. And now I found myself asking: is this all there is?

Her act over, Opal left the stage and materialized a few minutes later, working the room, moving languidly from table to table. When she reached mine she asked, "Is tonight a good night for a dance?" She leaned to touch my arm, letting the top of her blouse sag to reveal the pink margins of her nipples. Apparently she'd never learned that the coming attractions are no longer interesting once you've seen the movie. But her smile was friendly and charming, and I said, "Tell you what. I'll pay you for a dance if you just sit here and talk to me."

"Sure," she said. "Will you buy me a drink?"

I signaled the waitress. Opal ordered a Diet Coke. "This whole scene is new to me," I said. "I just want to talk."

"Sometimes that's what people do. It's fine. What's your name?"

"Homer," I said. "And I know yours is Opal. You are the only one who actually hangs upside down on the pole. Pretty impressive. I mean, I couldn't do that."

She laughed. "Thank you. We are always trying for working out different routines. It's hard to find something—fresh, I guess you could say. But we try. We don't want to be boring." She smiled, this time a little self-consciously, and I had the feeling a little of her real self was showing through. "So. What do you do, Homer?"

"I sell farm equipment," I said. I didn't know where that came from. Maybe some unconscious association with a name like Homer, but I was instantly sorry. I knew squat about farm equipment.

Her face lit up. "Oh? I grew up on farm, in Moldavia! Do you—?" Her face beamed as if I were a long, lost cousin, not knowing what to ask first. And I didn't even know where Moldavia was. "What kind of equipment do you sell?" She gazed expectantly.

I shrugged. "All kinds. Machinery, stuff for cows and horses."

"My parents had dairy farm in Moldavia. We had goats, too, for milking." She laughed as though it were a private joke. "You sell milking machines?"

"Sure. All kinds."

"Really? Oh my, how many kinds can there be?"

I shrugged. "There's your regular models and your deluxe models. The deluxe models cost more, but they, you know, get more milk out of the cow."

"Can you believe, we still milking by hand? Cows *and* goats?" She laughed again, shaking her dark hair away from her face, then laid an arm across the table as though offering to have blood drawn. "Here, feel this." Seeing my bewilderment, she took my hand, placed it on her forearm. "Go ahead, feel," she said, pressing my fingers around her arm. She opened and closed her fist, her muscles flexing powerfully. I decided I would not want to arm wrestle Opal. "You know, you think you finish cow, you give hands a rest, and ten minutes later? Bingo, more milk." She canted her head. "But of course you know all about that. You probably telling to your customers." Her smile was trusting.

"Right," I said. "Nothing does the job like a good milking machine."

She sipped her Coke, put down the glass. "You are first customer I meet who knows farming. Where are all the farmers in United States?"

"Dying breed," I said, with a forlorn shake of the head.

"In Moldavia, too." A flicker of sadness crossed her face. A little more of herself showing through.

"So what brings a nice farm girl from Moldavia to a place like this?" I said, monitoring her eyes.

I thought there was a shift, a hesitation before answering, but I couldn't be sure. "What do you think? Money," she said. "You cannot believe how poor Moldavian people are." She sipped her drink again, and over her shoulder I saw Tony, the bouncer from Club Belgrade, talking to the cashier at the front. He looked over and I slouched, but too late. He seemed unsure of what he saw, moved into the doorway and peered over at me. Then head lowered, he headed in my direction, coming on like a man with a purpose.

"The fuck you doing here?" he demanded.

I touched a finger to my lips. "Now, now, there's a lady present. But hey, why don't you join us? I'd introduce you, but I've forgotten your name."

He smacked both hands flat on the table, leaned close to my face and hissed, "Listen, motherfucker."

"Opal, Mr. Motherfucker." To him, I said, "Would Listen be okay? I feel kind of like we should be pals." I planted my feet on the floor, willed every muscle to relax, not knowing what he'd do next, not wanting to anticipate the wrong move. He seemed dumb enough to grab a fistful of my shirt, which would give me control of his dominant hand. But his arms were as big and solid as whiskey kegs. If he landed a halfway decent punch, I'd be down for the count.

But he surprised me. Still bent over his hands, he turned to face Opal. "You stupid cunt, get moving."

She got to her feet so quickly her chair banged onto the floor. "But Tony, I'm not—"

"Move!" he said, and she stalked away, almost stumbling on her stiletto heels, disappeared into the back room. Then Tony locked his eyes on mine, smiling with one half of his face. He didn't say anything more. He just turned and walked away.

I stayed around to watch the next couple of dancers, not because I wanted to, but because I wasn't going to let him run me out.

I went back to Earth Angels the following three nights. I didn't see Tony, but I didn't see Opal, either, and all the girls seemed to give me a lot of space. Not one came near my table.

The morning after that I was sitting at my desk looking out my office window and feeling like a pariah when the phone rang. It was Beth.

"Mike?" The sound of her voice came like a warm spring breeze after a thunderstorm. I thought of the corny old adage, "It's always darkest before the dawn." But her tone was cool and businesslike, and I realized things really could get darker. "I'm sorry for not calling you back, Mike," she said. "Stapler's fine. Would you like me to bring him back today?"

"No, no. But how about I drop by, pay you guys a visit? Tell you what, Beth. I'll pick you up and take you to lunch."

"I don't think so." Her tone was so cold it made my sinuses ache.

"Is something wrong?"

"I should have called you, Mike. I'm sorry, but—"

"Hey, no problem, you're forgiven," I said. *Stupid!* But she didn't respond. "What's the matter?"

She sighed. "Michael, Michael, Michael."

I waited. "What?"

"You'll never change. Look, it's really none of my business, it's just that, well—I've been deluding myself lately that maybe you'd grown up." Six second pause. "The night you dropped Stapler off?"

I waited. "Yeah?"

"I saw your car, Mike. And then I really needed to do some thinking, before I talked to you again. You will just never change, never grow up. And that's that."

"Saw my car? Beth, I don't know what you're talking about."

"Oh, I think you do. Look, I wasn't spying, but—the Gentleman's Club, Mike, I saw your car parked there, the night you dropped off Stapler. We drove right by that place, and there it was, you couldn't miss it, right next to the road, under all those lights. Or maybe somebody else drives an '84 Dodge Omni just like my old one."

"Beth, wait—"

"No, you wait. Listen, I'm not spying. I'm not, but now I can't help but look, whenever I drive by. You go there a lot, Mike."

"Beth, listen to me."

"No, you don't have to explain. And anyway, you're too much the lawyer, too quick and easy with words. Too good at manipulating me. Besides, there's nothing wrong with you going there anyway, not really. You're an adult. A free agent. I have no ties to you. You can spend your money any way you want to. It's just that I know you, and I can see you haven't changed, not one, single bit."

"Beth, listen. It's part of an investigation."

She laughed. "Great recovery, Mike! I've never known anyone who could think on his feet the way you do."

"No, Beth, listen."

"No, let's just not, okay? I'm sorry, I really am. Who am I to impose these, these, expectations on you? You are you. You will always be you. I'm sorry, Mike, it's really my own fault. I guess, for a while there, I started to allow myself to indulge in some— illusions. Foolish illusions."

"What kind of illusions?"

She laughed. It was a cruel laugh, and then she said goodbye and hung up.

I slumped back in my chair, swiveled around to look at her picture watching me from the credenza. Why the hell did I have to ask her about her illusions, go and change the subject when I should have been trying to explain? She probably thought my asking that was insufferably egotistical. Well, hell, it was. But what did she mean by illusions? That she'd been considering a rapprochement? What else could "illusions" mean? I picked up the phone to call her back, but hung up. Better wait, regroup, do it another time. I had an excuse to call her anyway. She still had my dog.

I called a florist instead, ordered a dozen roses. The guy took down all the information, and the last thing he asked was, "What would you like to put on the card?"

I thought about it a long time, groping for just the right sentiment.

"You still there?" he said.

"I'll call you back." Looking out on Washington Boulevard, I turned it over and over in my head. I never was any good at this. You can tell by the catchy name I thought up for my business: Legal Investigations, Inc. Or my dog: Stapler. Beth had always been the creative half of our union. Stapler, who I bought about a year after the divorce, went without a name for weeks. I just couldn't think of anything until a friend advised me to sit down, close my eyes, think pleasant thoughts, and the dog's name would be the first thing that came into my head. I shouldn't have done it while I was sitting at my desk.

Across from my office window, four costumed cheerleaders were bouncing along Washington Boulevard, probably coming from the Metra station and heading for an event at the Daley Center plaza. I turned away and looked directly into Beth's eyes. Was there a way to capture the depth of my longing for her on that note? Was that even a good idea? No; and anyway, she'd dismiss it as phony. Finally, hoping plain sincerity might win her over, I settled for this: "Beth—it really was an investigation."

It seemed right. I called the florist back and gave it to him, then spun my chair to the window again. Now a whole stream of cheerleaders poured down the sidewalk across the street, an explosion of color and perky frivolity, laughing and prancing in their miniskirts, some of their sweaters low-cut, all of them tight-fitting. All I could think was: *God, what wonderful tits!*

CHAPTER NINETEEN

After lunch I drove out to Mount Prospect and spent the afternoon staking out the apartment again, this time with a Scott Turow novel on tape. The entire day was fruitless.

The following morning started out cloudy and cold. This time I parked a little farther down the street, and slid a Joe Konrath mystery into the tape player. Konrath changed my luck. It went from bad to worse.

Beyond my windshield the sky began to brighten, clouds drifting away, and the sun's appearance felt like a good omen. Shortly afterward, two people left the building walking toward a Ford Focus, a woman in sunglasses and wide-brimmed hat, a guy in a black muscle shirt with a leather jacket slung over his shoulder. When they got closer, I saw that the woman was Opal, and there seemed to be something wrong with her face. I got out and walked quickly across the street, intercepting them just as Opal was reaching for the door.

"Opal," I said.

The guy, driver's door open and one foot inside, snapped his head around in my direction. It was the guy from the Wal-Mart parking lot, the one who held the girl's hand.

"Opal, are you okay?" I asked. She looked at me and her eyes went wide, her mouth opening into a horrified oval, her eyebrows lifted above her dark glasses. She screamed, "Get away from me, you creep!"

"Hey," the guy yelled, coming around the car. But I couldn't take my eyes off that turquoise bruise, an enormous blotch spreading across the swollen side of her face. I turned away too late, turned into the punch, took it square on the cheekbone, and went down. Instinctively I rolled away, tried to get to my feet but my head was full of vertigo, and he kicked me in the back and I went down once more. I curled into a fetal ball while he kicked me again and again, each blow harder than the last. I didn't try to get up. I thought he was never going to quit, and when he finally did, I stayed there, rolled up in that ball, hands clasped behind my head.

The engine started and the tires squealed off. I didn't move, just laid there a minute with the smell of burning rubber in my nose.

CHAPTER TWENTY

The next morning I awoke late, probably a result of the fistful of Vicodin I'd swallowed the night before. I hurt everywhere, and the fog of sleep gave way to rising anger. I got out of bed slowly, put on a pot of coffee, and limped down to the basement, hoping a little work on the heavy bag might loosen me up. But every jab delivered a knife blade of pain to my ribs, and finally I quit.

Back upstairs I sat at the kitchen table with a cup of coffee, wondering if I had a couple of cracked ribs—every breath hurt, even shallow ones. I considered going to the emergency room, but all they would do is tape up my ribs anyway, and I didn't have medical insurance.

Sitting there very still, I could not ward off dark thoughts of evening this score. I decided that what I needed was some sort of release, lest my anger fester to critical mass and lead to something really stupid. All too often, it worked that way.

Since I couldn't punch the bag, I could at least go to the pistol range and shoot lots of holes in paper targets that looked like the guy who'd kicked the shit out of me. I took a couple of pistols from my gun safe, dropped them in a range bag, and was on my way out the door when the phone rang. It was Lieutenant Verity.

"I tried your office," he said. "Glad I caught you, I got some information. Want to meet me for coffee somewhere?"

I wanted to hear what he had, but at the moment my greatest

need was to feel the gratifying recoil of a nine-millimeter pistol as I drilled holes through those silhouettes.

"I was just on my way to Maxon's, the pistol range in Des Plaines. Want to come along?"

"Hold on," he said. He must have covered the phone with his hand. I could hear him talking to his wife, then he came back. "Sure," he said.

Since I had to drive through Edison Park on the way to Maxon's, I told him I'd pick him up.

Half an hour later I pulled up in front of his house, a Chicago-style bungalow, yellow brick, the porch notched out of the building on one side. His wife invited me in, a plain-looking woman with intelligent eyes.

"I'm Ginny. Hank will be with you in a minute." This had to be the lady who followed Henry until he gave up the priesthood. She disappeared into the back of the house, and I found myself looking at two framed photos on the mantel over the fireplace, both of an adolescent boy, one kneeling in uniform holding a soccer ball. In the other he wore a more candid grin, hoisting a largemouth bass on the steps of a cottage somewhere, pine trees and the hint of a blue lake in the background. The kid had Verity's eyes and chin.

Hank came into the room carrying a paper sack. "That's my boy, Kevin," he said. "He goes to St. Juliana's. This one," he said, pointing to the fish picture, "was taken at our summer place, near Portage."

"Wisconsin?"

He nodded, then guiding me out the door, he said, "It used to be Ginny's folks' place." He slipped into the passenger's seat of my Omni. "Nice car."

"It was Motor Trend Magazine's 1984 car of the year," I told him as he struggled to close the door. "Here, sometimes that sticks." I reached across him and yanked it shut. "It was my first wife's car. When we split, I gave her my Lexus, and bought a Corvette. But I'm glad I hung onto this one. It's great for stakeouts, when you don't want to be sitting in a Corvette, drawing attention to yourself."

"Weren't you a lawyer then?"

"When I was divorced, yeah. Actually, I got married again. My second wife got the Corvette."

I drove down Touhy and turned onto Northwest Highway, waiting for him to tell me why he called. But the picture of his son with the fish led to talk about his summer cottage.

"You know, it's like a little bit of heaven, that place, getting away from it all. If I didn't have to live in the city—" His voice trailed off. "We are so blessed to have the place. We try to get up there as often as we can—luckily it's only about three hours, but a whole world away."

"My first wife wanted to buy a summer place," I said. "I was afraid it would be more work than fun."

"It's a lot of work, but you can make the work fun, too. Last fall I built a shed, so I could keep a couple of snowmobiles up there. We built it in one long weekend, just Kevin and me. I think I'll cherish that weekend for the rest of my life, just him and me working together. And I hope maybe Kevin will, too. He's so proud of that shed, you'd think we'd built the Taj Mahal. Makes you realize what life must have been like back in the old days, on family farms, the family all working together."

We spent about an hour at the range. Hank brought only his service pistol with one magazine in a paper bag, and we set up in adjoining booths, made a small wager for top score, loser buying lunch. Hank could really shoot. He emptied every magazine into a group no bigger than a baby's fist.

"Guess lunch is on me," I said, pulling onto Northwest Highway. We stopped at the Pickwick, the restaurant where I'd met Eva for a wee-hours' breakfast. After we ordered, I said, "You've got some information for me?"

"Right." He sat back in the booth. "It's about Club Belgrade—this is from a street source; confidential. The source says he knows for a fact that the partners owned the Demon Lover organization. That was their main source of income. Still is, for Vasil. They started Club Belgrade first, but now that's mainly a front. No big surprise there, huh?" He sipped his water, drew the back of a hand across his mouth.

"But here's the thing. About a year or two ago, some outfit in Wisconsin wanted to merge with Demon Lover. Or vice versa, I don't know who wanted to merge with who, but gentleman's clubs are becoming big in Wisconsin, they're sprouting up all over the place. Maybe it's because they can have total nudity there and still serve alcohol. Anyway, the story goes that they had a powwow, the Wisconsin guys and the Serbians, and the Serbians treated these Wisconsin owners like a bunch of hicks, finally told them to go fuck off. Right after that, Simunic got his."

I sat back. This could be a breakthrough, at least in light of the progress I was making. Or not making. "You know anything about this outfit?"

Before he could answer, the waiter brought our plates. Hank popped the top off a ketchup bottle and lathered his burger. "I know the main place is called Celestial Bodies. It's just outside of Westfield. Know where that is?"

"Sort of. You ever been to this place?"

"Not inside." He picked up his burger in both hands, took a bite, and from the corner of his mouth said, "I've driven by it. They've also got a porno shop right next door, I forget the name of it." He sipped his Coke and said, "You know, Mike, I got to share this with Violent Crimes."

I laughed. "Why should I care about that?"

He shrugged. "I'm just telling you."

I sat back and thought for half a minute. "Cutting off the hand, what do you think that's all about?"

He shrugged again, dabbed his mouth with a napkin and let his eyes rove the room. "I don't know, you're the homicide guy. Probably just a way of terrorizing Vasil. Leaving a horse's head on a pillow, that's been done."

Which set me thinking. "I don't remember—was the severed hand left at the scene?"

"Beats me. I was on furlough, up at the lake when it happened. Good point, though. But if they were going to use the hand, they would have used it by now."

"Maybe they did."

"Again, good point," he said. "From what I'm told, the partners acted like none of this was the business of the police. I could picture Vasil taking the hand from his pillow and dropping it down the garbage disposal." Then looking at me, his eyes came into focus. "By the way, I meant to ask you: what happened to your face?"

"Nothing. I walked into a door," I said. Then, because it seemed lame, I added, "I really need to get a night-light."

"You really did a job on yourself."

We turned onto Osceola toward Verity's house, the greening trees full of sunlight, kids swarming out of St. Juliana's Grammar School for the lunch hour. I parked in front, and Verity made no move to get out.

"Listen, Mike," he said. "You know what I'm doing is a little unorthodox."

He took it for granted that I would know what he meant, and

I did. A policeman, especially a lieutenant, going out of his way to assist a private investigator, getting all palsy-walsy. Maybe strictly speaking there were no rules against it, but it just wasn't done, and your average copper would look steeply down his nose at it. But Lieutenant Verity—nee Father Verity—was not exactly your run-of-the-mill copper, which sort of explained his odd remark about having to share the information with Violent Crimes.

"I was the one who told you, remember?" Hank said. "About white slavery being alive and well in Chicago? But no one believes it. We've got a moral obligation—" He corrected himself. "Well, I've got a moral obligation, anyway, it's a matter of conscience, and it keeps me awake at night. About the only thing I can do right now is try to help you."

Just then a freckle-faced boy with a backpack and a big smile crossed the lawn and stood at the passenger-side window, raised a palm Indian-style. "It's Kevin," Hank said, and tried to roll down the window. "How do you get this open?"

"It doesn't open," I said.

Verity cracked the door. "Kevin, this is Mr. Duncavan," he said. "He's a real, honest-to-God private eye."

Kevin said "Hi," snaked an arm through the crack and shook my hand. Then he said, "Dad, can we go up to the lake this weekend?"

Hank's eyes shifted to mine. Then to Kevin he said, "I'm working this weekend, kid. But maybe you and your mom can go."

CHAPTER TWENTY-ONE

I said goodbye and drove downtown to my office, a vague melancholy coming over me like a cloud shadow. I envied Verity's white-picket-fence life. For the last decade I'd longed for a child of my own, a longing keen with wonder. What would it be like to build something with your own son, to teach him things, to share things you know with him? To feel admiring eyes cast up at you? What would it be like to live in a real house where hearts might be made glad just by your coming home?

My next birthday would mark half a century on this planet, and I looked back on the wake of my life's passage, the flotsam of two failed careers, the jetsam of two failed marriages bobbing there, and I couldn't even turn my gaze to look ahead because I still yearned for my first wife. The single adornment of my office happened to be her picture on my credenza. My wanting her back had become the mortar of my existence. There wasn't much else holding me together.

Then I turned to wondering about who Verity's source was. Probably Wolfgang Bauer. Wolfy seemed a natural, had a view from the inside. He liked cops, and probably believed Verity could help him get on the police department. But I didn't trust Bauer—in my book he was as much a suspect as anyone. He was ambitious, and in light of his background with the East German police, probably unsentimental when it came to violence. And he had another motive—Eva said that the partners treated him like dirt, and Wolfy seemed the kind of guy who got even. A guy like me. My head still hurt, and pain shot through my ribs every time I took a deep breath. If there's to be any justice in the world, sometimes you need to shoulder the responsibility yourself.

I left my car at the parking garage and walked to the office wondering where to go from here, telling myself I could not let this get personal. I did want to talk to Eva a little more, maybe get a little insight on Wolfgang. And that Wisconsin place, Celestial Bodies. It was a long drive, but it was an obvious next step. And I couldn't deny it. What I wanted more than anything was a shot at the guy who kicked the hell out of me.

I usually take the stairs up to my second-floor office, but my ribs hurt and the elevator car was standing open in the lobby, so I got in and pressed the button, and when the doors opened I was treated to an odd sight: Tony, the bouncer from Club Belgrade, was crouched with his ear pressed against the keyhole of my office door.

"Can you hear the ocean?"

He scrambled to his feet with an agility you don't expect from someone that big, and faced me in that wrestler's posture, arms arcing from his sides. It was embarrassing. I was glad no one else was in the hallway.

"I got a message for you," he said.

I two-fingered a business card from my shirt pocket. "Here, next time phone it in."

He ignored the card. "This is the final warning," he said. "Stay out of his business."

"I'm sorry, you forgot to tell me who the message is from."

"Mr. Vasil, the boss. You know who it's from. You think you're bad, you little pissant? Listen, you just got in a lucky punch. I'm here to tell you, you ain't shit."

"Well, that's a relief," I said. "Would you like to come in?"

"Don't fuck with me. You're fucking with me, man, and I

don't like it."

"Wouldn't think of it," I said. Just then my office phone started to ring. "That it?"

He grunted, a little shift of uncertainty in his eyes, then walked wordlessly toward the elevator.

"Now I got a message for your boss," I said to his back. He turned. "When I find the Mexican who drives the van, I'm going to make him pray for death."

He gave me a strange look then. It was part pity, part appeal to reason. "Look, what's the matter with you, don't you know who you're messing with? I'm trying to help you," he said.

"Thank you kindly," I said. "And don't forget to deliver the message."

I waited until he got on the elevator and the door closed, then hurried to unlock the door, but before I reached the phone the answering machine kicked on. It was Orson Prescott, the claims adjuster.

I called him back.

"Mike, we need a progress report ASAP," he said. "Otherwise, I can't pay this bill. And, Mike, about the bill—you got time charges here for going to a Gentleman's Club?" He giggled. "This is a joke, right?"

I explained to him as well as I could what I'd learned so far, realizing as I spoke how pathetic was my progress. Orson listened politely. When I told him about Earth Angels, he said, "Mike, jeez, you need an assistant?" He giggled again. "Got to tell you, I'm an ass man, myself. But seriously. We can't pay you for time you spend in a goddamned Gentleman's Club. Jeez."

I was starting to steam. "It's part of the investigation."

"I know, I believe you, but it's—" He thought a moment. "Come on, Mike, you been around. This is an *insurance* company, for Christ sake. We got an image. What if it gets out that I was paying you to sit in a strip club and watch a bunch of broads get naked and shake their titties?"

The son of a bitch was arbitrarily cutting my bill. I slammed down the phone, went over to the sink, filled the coffeepot and started it brewing before it occurred to me that maybe I should not have hung up on my only client. I called him back. "Orson, Mike. What happened?"

"Dunno, I thought you hung up," he said.

"Sorry, been having trouble with my phones," I said. "I'll get you a status report within a week."

Chapter Twenty-Two

At eight-thirty the next morning, in the apartment above the tavern on Milwaukee Avenue, Bruno Malik rose, pulled on his bathrobe and went into the kitchen. He hadn't gone to bed until three-thirty that morning, his usual hour after he closed the tavern, and as usual, he had hardly slept. Now he longed for the escape that just a single night's sleep would bring. One good, single night's sleep, that's all it would take, and he'd wake up and maybe see his life as something worth living. But insomnia had robbed him of rest, of distraction, for as long as he could remember.

Eleanor was not at home, but she'd left half a pot of cold coffee in the coffeemaker. He took a coffee cup from a rack of dishes on the sink and washed it again. In thirty-two years of marriage, Eleanor never washed dishes right. Always they were greasy; always they had bits of dried food clinging to them, or lipstick. Though Bruno no longer cared whether the cup was clean or dirty—there really wasn't anything he cared about, now—he washed it again out of habit.

He heated a cup of coffee in the microwave, then as he sat drinking it at the kitchen table, he heard Eleanor and Cindy's footfalls coming up the back stairway, Cindy chattering away. When the two came through the back door into the kitchen, Eleanor's eyes skipped past him as though he were another kitchen appliance, but Cindy fell silent when she saw him, stood inside the door and stared.

"You can't say hello to your father?" he said.

"Come, come." Eleanor took her arm and led her past him toward the front of the apartment.

There was a time when Bruno would not have let Eleanor get away with that, ignoring him, disrespecting him. Then he would have yelled after her: "Hah! Who *is* her father, anyway?" There was a time when he might even have grabbed Eleanor by the arm, told her she could not treat him with such disrespect. But then she would only stare into his eyes with that mocking grin, knowing he would go no further. Bruno had never actually struck her. She deserved it; a thousand times, she deserved it. But now, though Bruno could muster the hatred, he could no longer muster the energy.

Twice now, he had loaded a single chamber of his revolver, spun the cylinder, slipped the cold barrel between his lips, and pulled the trigger. Twice, he'd heard only that irritating snap. One day he would do it, and he would hear no sound at all. There would be nothing more than peace, forever. Why then don't I load all the chambers? What am I hanging on to, when all I want is peace?

But he knew his dying would only make Eleanor happy, set the slut free. Well, there was a way to do it, and make her sorry. So, so sorry, she would be, inconsolable. He would kill himself, and he would make Eleanor suffer for the rest of her life, make her wish she was dead, too.

CHAPTER TWENTY-THREE

The next day I called Henry Verity and told him I was driving up to Westfield, Wisconsin, to have a look at Celestial Bodies.

"You'll practically drive by our cottage. It's only about twenty miles south of Westfield. Why don't you stay there?" I listened while he gave me directions, though I had no intention of using his place. "There's a key under a rock," he said, "just to the right of the front porch."

Interstate 90 was wide open all the way. Having made better time than I expected, it was still light when I pulled into the parking lot at Celestial Bodies. The club wasn't open yet, but the porno shop next to it was, its sign touting in foot-high letters:

Gifts and Gags for Gals and Guys Galore.

I avoided eye contact with the clerk behind the cash register, moved out of her line of sight into an aisle surrounded by more sexual devices than I thought possible. There were cupid lips attached to a soft, flesh-colored tube for a self-administered blow job; a variety of inflatable women with orifices touted to feel "just like the real thing." There was some sort of plastic circular device that fit around gonads to maximize pleasure. For the ladies there were giant dildos that not only vibrated but played a selection of romantic tunes. One device was a flat gizmo shaped like a lite-days pad. It came with a remote control activator so a needful lady could wear it in her panties and get off while riding the bus.

Not altogether comfortable, I'd stayed long enough. I headed for the door with my eyes cast down, the fat girl trilling from the register, "Come back soon." I turned just enough to nod to her, and caught sight of a sign on the counter:

CLEARANCE ON HANDCUFFS
Two pairs, $6.95.

Stacked in flat boxes, a single pair was on display, and without thinking I picked it up, examined it. Tinny, shoddy, without craftsmanship. In the old days a good pair of handcuffs, Smith and Wesson or Peerless, say, went for about fifty bucks. You wouldn't want to carry these on the street, but then, they were obviously made for the bedroom. And they seemed to work okay. "I'll take two," I said. She put them in a pink paper bag spotted with cupid lips.

I still had time to kill. With nothing else to do, I turned back south on I-39, got off at an exit near Portage and went looking for Verity's cabin. After some false starts and backtracking down rural roads I located the driveway, just a couple of sandy tracks the color of buckskin leading into the woods. It snaked through oaks and jack pines, and I surprised a flock of wild turkeys scratching in the dirt. They melted into the trees and then the cedar buildings came into view.

I mounted the steps to the porch, tried peering under the drawn window shade, but the interior was dark. The storage shed, cedar-sided to match the cabin, stood nearby like a fawn following its mother. Behind the cabin a footpath dropped down to a small lake, a plank pier jutting onto the water. It was all so peaceful. The oaks were pushing out green buds, and everywhere were signs of spring. I stood at the brow of the hill for a long time, a hummingbird now and then zipping past my head to a feeder, and watched the sun drop into the trees across the lake. When the call of a whippoorwill started echoing on the water, I drove back to Celestial Bodies.

It was dark by the time I got there, the lights of the club flaring up out of the woods, the parking lot overflowing with cars and pickup trucks.

The place was spacious, a bar on the right and a stage on the left. The cover charge was only five bucks, and I took a stool at a high, round table with my back to a window. A few guys in their twenties were sitting along the edge of the stage.

I sipped Stoli and watched the show, the dancers a little more athletic than those at Earth Angels, inspired perhaps by the music, mainly hip-hop, the lyrics distinctive, monomaniacal.

"Your pussy is the sweetest thang that I ever see-ee. I wanna see your pussy, show it to mee-ee!"

Then there was, "My pussy is the hippest thing around—that's right!"

And my personal favorite, "I bring my pussy with me, where ever I go-oh." (Imagine!)

Dance over, the girls would leave the stage and stand naked with the customers at a corner of the bar for a few minutes, then pull on some skimpy clothing and move off to work the room. The ambiance was different from Earth Angels, sort of country casual. A flyer on a bulletin board near the front door advertised a Wild Game Feed and Gun Raffle at the Westfield Sportsman's Club.

After about half an hour, one of the girls came over to my table, about twenty-five, silver cowboy boots, silver hot pants, and a short, see-through vest. "Hi, I'm Amber, did you like my dance?"

"Terrific," I said.

"You can put a tip right in here," she said, bringing her upper arms together to compress her breasts, pointing to her cleavage.

"Here, give me your hand." I put a single in her palm.

"Oh, you are so swee-eet," she trilled. She kissed my cheek and climbed onto a stool.

"Would you like a drink, Amber?"

"Oh, you are so swee-eet," she echoed, and by her glassy eyes I sensed we weren't going to have an intelligent conversation.

The bartender brought her a rum and Coke, and while we made small talk a dancer named Melody took the stage, moving to a rhythm three times faster than a human heartbeat. She looked older than the rest, with big, intelligent eyes. She swung a foot high above her head, hooked a heel onto the pole, hung upside down and spiraled to the floor, her hair swinging in a wide arc, the music hammering. *"You be drinkin' my blood, while I be lickin' your wounds."*

"Do you like my tits?" I turned to Amber, who was studying her reflection in the window behind us, her top tugged down, her chin bunched. "I think my nipples are—" I could not make out her slurred words over the music.

"I'm sorry, I didn't hear you."

She shouted now, enunciating. "I think . . . my . . . nipples . . . are . . . too . . . far . . . apart." The music stopped. "You think I should get them fixed?"

"They look fine to me."

Then she slapped her cheek and said, "Oohmygod, I follow Melody." She knocked back the rum and Coke and was gone.

Melody left the stage and took a place at the end of the bar for a few minutes, then pulled on a gauzy blouse and crossed the room to my table. "Hi, are you tipping the ladies tonight?"

"I am. Would you join me?" I gave her a twenty, and she climbed onto a stool. "How about a drink," I said.

"No thanks. I don't drink."

"It might help some of your co-workers to follow your example."

"I know, I saw Amber sitting with you. I hope she didn't embarrass herself. I cut her off earlier. You might have guessed, I'm the oldest one here." She grinned. "I've turned into the mom, you could say."

"You're certainly the most athletic."

She laughed and groaned at the same time. "It's catching up with me. By the end of the night I feel it. I don't think I've seen you in here before. What's your name?"

"Homer," I said, this time intending to be an insurance salesman, if the subject came up.

"Homer, will you excuse me? I've got to mingle," she said.

I watched her go, then scooped up my change and left.

I went back the next two nights, tipping Melody generously for talking with me. She was hot, no doubt about that, yet from that first moment she approached my table, she never flaunted her body like the others. Probably she'd sized me up, knew that strip club flirtations didn't do it for me, and played the role she thought would fulfill my fantasies. If so, she had me pegged. Melody was easy to talk to, and with her English Lit. degree—if she really had an English Lit. degree—she certainly didn't fit the stereotype. She talked mostly about her failed marriage, about her kids and how hard it had been raising them, about the long commute from Milwaukee. It was the sort of exchange you might have with a co-worker.

Before she'd come to Celestial Bodies she was working at a club outside of Milwaukee, but when a guy she went to high school with came in she decided the place was too close to home and started commuting here, a ninety-mile drive each way. "But it's worth it," she said. "I've got two kids in high school, so I don't want to be working anywhere near home.

Besides, the bosses here are the nicest guys in the world—that's a big factor. What do you do, Homer?"

"I'm a writer," I said, in what I thought was an amazing piece of footwork, a spur-of-the-moment calculation that really I knew less about insurance than I did about farm machinery. I didn't know much about writing, either, but it would be easier to fake, and give me an excuse for asking a lot of questions.

Her eyes brightened. "Oh? What kind?"

"Mysteries," I said. "Just crass commercial fiction. Actually, that's why I'm here, I'm doing a little research. This whole scene is all new to me," I said.

"What are you writing about?" she said.

"It's about a murder in a club, like this one." I took a fifty-dollar bill from my wallet, tucked it in her palm. "This is yours, regardless. But I really need a consultant on this. Will you help me?"

She put the fifty back in my hand. "We don't date the customers, Homer."

"No, no date. How about if I call you?"

"Sorry, we don't give out phone numbers, either."

"You call me, then. Melody, take the fifty now, it's yours. You decide not to call me, fine. If you call me, I'll give you another fifty."

There was an uncertain shift in her eyes, figuring no doubt that the second payment would require personal contact. "I'll bring it to the club," I said, placing the fifty on the table in front of her. She looked at it, then at me.

"I'll have to clear it with the boss."

"Roger?" I asked.

"No, Darryl. Who's Roger?"

"I thought the owner's name was Roger."

"No, Darryl Stamphley's the owner." She squinted at me, wondering where "Roger" came from.

I shrugged.

"Darryl's been terrific. But he's got his rules, and I don't want to do anything like that without checking with him."

I guessed I had nothing to lose. "Deal," I said. "Here's my number. Call me tomorrow morning?"

"Tomorrow afternoon," she said. "About one o'clock."

She didn't call until nearly two and when she did she apologized, said she'd had an appointment with her son's teacher during the lunch hour. "I didn't get home from the school until just now," she said. "So. Tell me about your novel."

I told her I was writing about some dancers who were brought from Europe on the promise of getting office jobs, then were held as virtual slaves, forced to dance, forced into prostitution. I was certain that wasn't her situation. Still, she'd have some insight, and I was sorry I couldn't watch her facial expression.

When I finished she just said, "Interesting idea."

"Is it believable?"

"You'd have to suspend a lot of disbelief." Maybe she really did have an English Lit. degree.

"What do you mean?"

"Dancers make really good money. Far more than they could make doing anything else. I mean, take my case—where do you go with my degree? So I doubt they need to be forced."

"But what if they're not getting any of the money. What if they're captives?"

"They're in America. Why wouldn't they just walk away?"

"So you don't think it's possible?"

She hesitated. "Depends on how you write it, I guess. If people buy into a world of Hobbits, I suppose they could buy into all that."

"What do you think about the prostitution angle?" I might have been treading on shaky ground, here. I didn't know whether the girls at Celestial Bodies went that far, but it seemed only one short step for womankind.

"Prostitution's illegal," she said. "I wouldn't know anything about it." Letting me know I'd crossed a line.

"Melody, I'd really like to get Darryl's angle on this. Do you think he'd talk to me?"

She laughed. "Are you going to pay him, too?" Then without waiting for an answer, she said, "He probably would. He's a great guy. Want me to ask him?"

"I'd appreciate it."

CHAPTER TWENTY-FOUR

At the club that night I gave Melody the fifty I owed her. She told me Darryl agreed to talk with me. "You'll like him, he's really a sweetie. He said to drop by the office any time after two tomorrow."

At ten minutes to two the next day, one other car stood in the parking lot. Darryl answered the door, a big man with a big smile in a pink face, his red hair thinning and mostly gray, a little shaggy around the collar. His sandpaper hand closed around mine like a fielder's glove. He ushered me to a back office. The window looked out on a slope of green pasture dotted with black-and-white cows. In the distance the top of a silo rose up behind a hill.

"You know," Darryl said, "if a fella wanted to, he'd be free to use the name of Celestial Bodies in his book. The publicity couldn't hurt."

"I can do that. How long have you been in business, Darryl?"

"Only about four years," he said. "My cousin opened a place in Milwaukee. He did pretty well, and I thought it could work here, too. So we opened this one together. We got girls from all around. Treat 'em right, they treat you right. Some come from pretty far, so we got an apartment we let them stay in if they want to, for minimal rent. Hell, it don't even cover our cost, but some of the girls come all the way from Manitowoc and Appleton, even Milwaukee. We're open seven days, and some of the girls, they work kind of like firemen. On one, off two. But, hey,

I'm talking too much. How can I help you?"

"No, that's just what I need, Darryl, the flavor of the operation. But you can tell me this: do you think your operation is any different than the ones in the city?"

"Like how?"

I shrugged. "Your girls seem pretty happy. Think it's that way everywhere?"

It was his turn to shrug. "Like I say, you treat them right, they treat you right. Other than that, I couldn't say."

"Did Melody tell you about my idea for a story? About girls being forced to work against their will?"

"Yes, she did tell me that."

"Think that ever happens, Darryl?" I was watching his eyes; they betrayed nothing.

"Don't want to hurt your feelings," he said, "but it seems a little far-fetched to me."

"No, that's the kind of thing I need to hear. Darryl, have you ever heard of an organization called 'Demon Lover'?"

This time there was a definite shift in his eyes. "Yes, why do you ask?"

"What can you tell me about them?"

"Well I—" He exhaled and looked at me silently. Then he said, "Mike, you're really not a writer, are you?"

"Sure I am."

"Why are you asking me about Demon Lover?"

"I was doing a little research down around Chicago. That's how I got the name of your outfit."

"Let me tell you something. You're more fulla shit than a Texas outhouse. Now tell me why you're asking me these questions."

I decided to lay it on the table. I apologized for misleading him, confessed that I was investigating two deaths for the insurance company. I gave him the names of the deceased partners.

When I finished he said, "I guess I probably ought to throw you out of here. Insurance company, huh? That the truth?"

I showed him my blue card, which at least established my identity as a private investigator. "Darryl, it can't hurt to talk to me. There are unsolved murders. Now I got information that you had some kind of business dealings with Demon Lover. If you clam up and something breaks, down in Chicago, next thing you know the cops could be sniffing all around this place. That's the kind of publicity you don't need."

He stared at me levelly for several seconds and lowered his eyes. When he looked at me again, he said, "I don't know anything about Demon Lover, other than my cousin in Milwaukee talked about maybe hooking up with them somehow. We talked to the one guy, Milan Krunic? You say he's dead?"

"He and his partner, Uri Simunic. Both murdered."

"Well, I won't be shedding any tears. Look, we met with those guys. They acted like real jerks, like their shit didn't stink. Like we was beneath them, just a buncha hicks. And here they are, a bunch of goddamned DP's from nowhere. Fuckers couldn't even speak English, not very good, anyway."

"And what happened then?"

"Nothing happened then. That ended it." He pushed his chair back and crossed his leg. "Damn, I got sciatica, I can't sit long." He stood then, hobbled to the window, studied the dairy herd a moment, returned and sat down. "I never knew in the first place why Junior—that's my cousin—why he ever wanted to get mixed up with them."

"Do you know anything about their business?"

"Other than they seemed to have a lot of clubs, and seemed to be doing pretty damn good." He pulled a knee to his chest, then put his foot on the floor and leaned toward me. "Wait a minute. Are you trying to say that they're holding girls against their will?"

"Could they be?"

"Like I told you before, I can't see how that's possible. But if anybody ever done that, those guys are just the type of scum you'd expect to do it."

The drive back on I-90 seemed twice as long as the drive up. I wondered whether to believe Darryl. I abide by the old journalist's maxim: If your mother says she loves you, check it out. Still, the guy seemed like the genuine article. My hunch was that the abortive merger idea was just a coincidence, that Celestial Bodies had no connection to Demon Lover, let alone the murders. His description of the partners' behavior fit perfectly with Dave Donavan's, the insurance agent. Which meant this was probably a wasted trip. And that the insurance company probably wouldn't pay me for it. I was no further ahead than when I started. I toyed with the idea of calling Orson Prescott at Minnesota Mutual and telling him I was giving it up.

The trouble with long drives is that if something's eating at you, it's got a lot of time to make serious headway. The boredom of the darkening open road, the aches from sitting in the same position, the sore spots where the Mexican had kicked the shit out of me, provided fertile soil for the germination of black thoughts.

Cops have this little secret. When someone puts a serious hurt on you, line of duty or not, it's personal. Societal rules may say otherwise, but it's not society's skin, it's your own.

I remember a story that went around, back when I was a homicide detective, about a guy named Price who worked out of robbery down the hall. Price was an older black guy, a copper's copper. Though I never knew Price well, I sort of idolized him.

The story, true or not, went like this. Price was canvassing a neighborhood, looking for leads on a guy wanted on an armed robbery warrant. He's knocking on all kinds of doors, and then he knocks on one and who opens it but the guy he's looking for. Price is alone, so he draws his pistol, backs the guy up into the living room, tells him to turn around, and snaps on one cuff. Then he holsters his revolver so he can get the other cuff on, but the guy jerks away and snatches a pistol of his own, from behind a picture frame. He's got Price dead to rights, who's standing there with his gun holstered and his hands up, and he just raises his hands, backs away and says, "Okay, don't shoot." But the guy does shoot. He shoots from the hip, six times, empties his gun. But he misses Price every time. Now the stickup guy throws down the empty gun, raised his hands and says, "I give up." Then—or so the story goes—Price says, "Oh no you don't." He draws his revolver and shoots the guy dead on the spot. "Now," Price says over the bleeding corpse. "Now's your turn to give up, Chump."

I love that story. Whose rules did Price break? The only two in the game were Price and the stickup man, and Price was only playing by the stickup man's rules. When the stickup guy missed every shot, he retired the side, and it was Price's turn. The guy simply handed his future over to Price. A very limited future. It wasn't society's business; maybe it wasn't even God's. It was between Price and the bad guy.

Now my thoughts kept swinging like a compass needle to the Mexican and how I'd let him kick the piss out of me. That was personal. Was I going to let him get away with it? The steam inside me grew with every passing mile, the reasoning part of Mike Duncavan leaping and waving from the sidelines, trying to get my attention. *Let it go, you're supposed to be all grown up now,* the little man said. I listened to him, sort of. By the time I reached Chicago, we had fought to a draw.

★ ★ ★ ★ ★

The next morning there was a message from Beth on my answering machine. "The roses are beautiful, Mike. Stapler said to tell you he misses you. Please call us, okay?"

I hit the playback button, listened to it again. Then I took off my coat and sat at my desk replaying it over and over, mentally caressing every syllable, sifting the words for any underlying messages. It seemed straightforward, free of baggage. But that was how Beth was: wonderfully uncomplicated.

I called her back. She seemed genuinely delighted. "Thank you again for the roses," she said in that slow, sexy way she sometimes spoke, and again I savored the words. But that was it—that was all she said.

"You're welcome," I said, and did not know what else to say.

She said, "So."

"Beth," I said.

"What?"

"I'd like to see you."

Now the silence was palpable. Finally, she said, "Oh, Mike." She didn't say anything then. I gave it a decent interval. "People change, Beth. I've changed. What do you say we just—have dinner or something?"

"I don't know."

"Dinner, what can it hurt?"

"Me. It can hurt me, Mike. I've got to move on with my life. Besides—"

I waited for her to finish, and when she didn't, it was my turn to say, "What?"

"There's—someone else in my life, now."

I don't know why that came as such a blow. I slumped in my chair, my forehead turning damp. My hands may have even trembled a little. I said, "Hey, remember when you said we'd always be married in the eyes of the Lord?"

153

"I can't believe you're bringing that up again. Do you remember when you said, 'People change?' It was about one minute ago."

Two things she said loomed in my mind, opposing each other like a pair of gladiators. On one hand, she said there was someone new in her life. But on the other, she hesitated—at least I thought she did—when she said "I don't know" to my dinner invitation. "I don't know" is definitely not "no." That seemed like an opening, maybe not much of one, but big enough for the small end of the wedge.

"So what you're saying is, you're a free woman. Which means you're still free to have dinner with me."

She laughed then, an unguarded laugh that surged through me like joy mainlined, and when she didn't answer I said, "At least think about it, Beth?"

She chuckled. "Okay."

"You're not just putting me off, now."

"No, I'll think about it. But that's all, no promises."

I hung up and stared at her picture for a full minute, then too elated to sit still, I danced around my desk, picked up the picture and kissed it, then I went to the window and looked down upon the little knot of mere mortals waiting for the light to change so they could cross Wells Street. Beth and I had come close to getting together before. During my work on the hyena case, we saw each other regularly. But I'd made a mistake, inadvertently got her involved in that one, which I regretted. Yet for a short time it brought us close. Could I really commit to her, even now?

I still had a weakness for women. It occurred to me that, in an age when TV ads tout remedies for erectile dysfunction, someone should be hawking a pill for a person like me—a schmuck with the opposite problem.

Even when I really began to miss Beth after the divorce, I

still knew that if she took me back, I probably wouldn't be able to control my urge to stray. I saw then that, no matter how devoted I was to her, sooner or later I would slip. I accepted the fact that I just wasn't built for monogamy.

But now, nearing the fifty-year mark, I believed I really *had* changed. Those nights in the gentleman's clubs, all those lovely creatures—for me their feminine mystery vanished with the shedding of their garments, and my libido seemed shot through with Novocain.

Now standing at my window overlooking Wells Street, a simple idea came to me with such power I reeled a little. I would prove to myself, before making any promises to Beth, that I could remain celibate for—how long? Three months. A Biblical season. If I could remain celibate until mid-July, I'd be girded for battle, ready to fight to win Beth back.

At home that evening, I microwaved a pair of Hungry Man dinners, feeling pretty good about my resolve. I ate them with a couple of beers in front of the TV, then slipped *Casablanca* into the VCR, and fell asleep before Claude Raines said how shocked he was to find gambling at Rick's. I dreamed of Beth, of having her back in my bed, and for the first time in more than three decades, a wet dream exploded my loins and wakened me.

CHAPTER TWENTY-FIVE

After working out on the speed bag and the heavy bag the next morning, I got on my bike and pedaled fast over to Humboldt Park, and fueled by thoughts of Beth, zoomed along the web of asphalt paths, then raced home. In the old days I'd been a dedicated runner, jogged about four miles a day, but a bullet through the ankle ended that. Now if I even walk fast, the ankle starts throbbing. I can still sprint half a block if I absolutely have to, but at the cost of a couple days' limping, and heavy doses of Ibuprofen.

I showered, was about to sit down at the kitchen table with newspaper and coffee when the phone rang.

"Did you see the morning paper?" Marty Richter asked.

"It's sitting here still in the plastic. Why?"

"That bag of money turned up, the one that was taken from Milan Krunic the morning he was murdered."

"Bag of money. You mean all the money was still in it?"

"Yeah, turned up in a church," he said.

"Hang on." I pulled the plastic sleeve off the paper, located the story on page seven. "So what do you think?"

"Same thing I always thought. The motive wasn't robbery. Seems pretty clear now, doesn't it?"

I said goodbye and read the short article. Father Koulogeorge, pastor of Visitation Parish on the south side, discovered the bag of money in a storage room in the church basement. As far as anyone could tell, all the money was still there.

The article was short, with few details, and I called Visitation Parish. The housekeeper said Father Koulogeorge was saying the eight o'clock Mass, but she expected him back shortly.

"Will he be around for a while after Mass?"

"I don't know. He'll be here for breakfast," she said. "Otherwise, I don't know what his schedule is."

I dressed fast and got in the car and headed out to the south side church. The Kennedy wasn't too bad, considering it was the morning rush, and I actually breezed past the Loop exits, but an accident on the Dan Ryan brought movement to a crawl. I should have waited to talk to the priest on the phone, made an appointment. But patience was never my strong suit. I dialed the rectory on my cell phone, asked for Father Koulogeorge again.

"He's eating breakfast," the housekeeper said. "Can I take a message?"

It wasn't the kind of thing that fit well into a message. "No, thank you."

Fifteen minutes later, I turned onto tree-shaded Garfield Boulevard, and as I neared Green Street the turquoise top of the steeple loomed above the trees, the yellow stone facade warming in the sun.

I gave my card to the elderly black lady who came to the rectory door, and asked to see Father Koulogeorge. She wanted to know if I had an appointment. I told her no. She silently led me to a small parlor, sat me in a comfortable chair, and left me there.

The priest came in a few minutes later wearing a short-sleeved Hawaiian shirt, a little overweight with a roll of fat around his chin, his black, wavy hair peppered with gray. His eyes, friendly and uncurious, made me think that unscheduled visits might not be unusual. I stood.

"Mr. Duncavan?"

157

I nodded. "Mike," I said. "Mike Duncavan."

"How can I help you?" He gestured for me to sit, closed the door, and took a seat behind the writing desk.

I started to tell him that I was investigating the Krunic murder for the insurance company, but before I could finish he interrupted.

"I've already told the police everything I know."

"Well, I'm a private investigator. The police aren't good at sharing."

He laughed, seemed to relax a little, and related the events in a rote way. He'd told this story a number of times. The parish kept a bin in the parking lot where people could donate discarded clothing or odds and ends for the "Book Bag Store," a resale shop whose proceeds went to buy books for poor kids. The project was started by a former assistant pastor years earlier. Every few days Alvin Crown, a part-time employee, emptied the bin and carried the contents to a storage room in the church basement. "Alvin is—slow," he said. "Down's syndrome. Apparently he found the bag of money in the bin at some point, and just put it in the basement along with the clothing."

"Can I talk to Alvin?"

"I'd rather you didn't," he said. "He's very frightened of the police."

"I'm not—"

"I know. All the same, I'd rather not subject him to any more of this. For some reason, he's gotten the idea he did something wrong. The police have already talked to him, and that has put him in kind of a state."

"Do you have any idea how long the bag was in there?"

"As I said, we check the bin every other day or so, so it wouldn't have been in *there* too long. But I found it buried under a lot of clothing in the storeroom, so I have no idea how long it was down there. Probably a while. But Alvin said—said to me—that he doesn't remember putting it in there. He wouldn't say anything to the police. He doesn't understand, he's not really able to deal with this very well, and I don't want to pressure him any further."

"And you have no idea who might have put it there?"

"None," he said. He smiled and stood and extended his hand, letting me know that the interview was over.

CHAPTER TWENTY-SIX

Back in my office, I sat at the window contemplating my next move. I came up empty, so I decided to call Eva. She was my best link to Stepan Vasil's organization. I hadn't talked to her since that night at the Pickwick Restaurant. She seemed happy to hear from me which, given my lack of progress, felt pretty good. I asked her if she'd be free for dinner one evening, and suddenly I became aware that my interest might not be entirely professional. I have a way of fooling myself.

"Is this business or pleasure?" Perceptive. She'd hit on the very question of the moment.

Then I remembered my commitment to celibacy. "Can it be both?" I wasn't sure which, business or pleasure, would be most productive, case-wise. The pleasure part, after all, could just as well be platonic.

"We-ell," she said.

I waited.

"Okay, why not."

Back at my apartment that evening, I pulled on a navy turtleneck and gray blazer and was nearly out the door when it occurred to me that I was unarmed. My license allowed me to carry a weapon while I was working, or traveling to and from. Business or pleasure? I went back to my bedroom, slipped off the blazer, and slipped on a shoulder holster with a .357 Colt revolver.

At seven I knocked on Eva's door, an apartment on the

second floor of one of those California-style buildings with an open balcony and wrought-iron railings. She was ready, came to the door in a playful mood, and as we walked to the car I was once again smitten by the way she carried herself. Sensuality smoldered from the most ordinary gesture. She was probably past the forty-year mark, but she would still turn heads.

We drove to Cafe Lucci on Milwaukee Avenue near Central, a place with white tablecloths and a touch of elegance. I ordered a Stoli on the rocks, she ordered the same, a double, and as the waiter started to walk away she repeated the routine of ordering two at a time.

"Two doubles?" he asked.

"Yes," she said.

When he was gone, she said, "You probably think I drink too much." She didn't let me answer. "But I don't. You know I tend bar all night and I never touch a drop? Not one. Not when I'm working." A trace of irritation had come into her voice, her cheerfulness seemed to be evaporating. She lit a cigarette, turned her head away and blew a plume of smoke. "I have not had a very good life, Mike Duncavan."

I sat back. This could get touchy. The waiter brought our drinks, and when he was gone I said, "Do you want to talk about it? Your life?"

"No." Then looking past me her eyes grew narrow and burned with private thoughts. "I could die if I talk about it," she said matter-of-factly. She lifted her glass and drank, then put it down and looked into my eyes as though expecting me to react. I didn't say anything. She finished one Stoli, picked up the second, and laid impatient eyes on the waiter, who was taking an order at a nearby table.

"Do you want to order?" I asked.

"No," she said. The waiter turned away from the other table

161

and she waved to him. "One more."

"Double?"

"Yes, double." She looked at me. "Another?"

"Thanks, later."

"So." She sat back, her eyes probing mine. "You think I'm kidding, that I could die for what I tell you?"

I shook my head.

"And you aren't curious about that?"

"Sure I am. But I think you'll tell me what you want to tell me when you're ready."

She was rubbing her glass on the tablecloth and looking into the distance, then her head started nodding in syncopation with the movement of her hand. When she looked at me again, her eyes were already a little glassy. The vodka was taking hold, and I wasn't sure that was good.

"These people, they have stolen my life," she said. "They are pigs."

I leaned on my arms, waiting for her to say more.

"Shall we order now?" she said.

We looked at the menus and ordered, and Eva said, "Did you ever hear of Stepan Vasil? Before, I mean."

"Before?" I shook my head.

"Before he came here. He was a big shot in the war, in Bosnia. Why they allow him in this country, I don't know. In Bosnia, they are wanted for war crimes, I think. All of them."

"All of who?"

"All of the partners, but Stepan—he is the worst one. An evil, sick man." Her eyes went to the tablecloth.

I gave it a moment and asked, "Evil in what way?"

Her eyes came back into mine, deciding something. "Never mind," she said. "I am wrong for saying this. He is my life."

When she went quiet again, I said, "Can I ask you what you mean by that? He's your life?"

She shook her head. "I didn't say that," she said.

It was getting strange, and I let the silence go on, and in a little while she said, "I meant, I owe him my life. He's been very good to me." She lifted her prosthetic hand. "Who wants to hire someone like this? Please, I don't want to talk about Stepan Vasil anymore."

"Okay," I said. "But do you mind if I ask you about something else?"

"Go ahead," she said absently.

"Demon Lover, what can you tell me about it?"

She looked at me, her mouth coming open a little, and before she could answer, I said quietly, "I know all about it, Eva, I've been to Earth Angels, I've seen Tony bringing the girls back and forth to the club. I think you know what's going on there."

She gave me a weary look, then mocked me with her smile. "You don't know what you're talking about. So what's going on there? You tell me."

"Those girls—they're prisoners, aren't they?"

"Are they? You tell me," she said again, a little belligerent now. I was pushing her, and I needed to back off.

"We're here to have a good time," I said. "Let's talk about something else."

The waiter brought our food, and her mood improved with the meal and the wine. We talked about movies, and afterward we ordered coffee and cognac, and then she covered my hand with hers. "Take me home now, Mike?" Her eyes were beautiful, and I was sure they were hungry.

At her front door she rummaged through her purse. "Shit," she said, then bent and lifted the door mat, uncovering a key. She opened the door, and tucked the key back under the mat.

Eva's apartment was all glass and chrome and hardwood floors. Even the couch, where I sat while she was putting Ella Fitzgerald on the CD player, seemed rigid. She disappeared into the kitchen, returned in a couple of minutes carrying two drinks. She handed me one, then sat next to me with her legs drawn up under her and played a finger through my hair.

"I really like you, Michael Duncavan. I wish you never got involved in this."

"What am I involved in?"

"Nothing. I mean, involved in anything to do with Stepan and the rest."

"Could you be a little more specific?"

"No. Drink," she ordered, and tinked her glass to mine. She tilted it to her lips and drained it, then set the empty glass on the coffee table. She moved against me, draped her arms around my neck, brought her parted lips to mine and kissed me deeply, pressed her body against mine, her kisses deep and quick and insistent. I drank her in, all of her, her ripe body, the smell of her hair, her cologne.

Then she stood and took my hand and led me to her bedroom and we undressed in the light from the open door, her breasts round and splendid and edged in curving light, and still standing she pressed her nakedness against me and pulled my face to hers and covered me again with impatient kisses, and then she pulled me onto the bed, pulled me onto her, then with a moan, into her, her pelvis driving now, urgent. I fought to hold back but exploded inside her.

I rolled onto my back, and she turned on her side and drew herself against me, cradling her head on my shoulder.

"Sorry," I said.

She laughed. "My fault. You're too magnificent." She touched my chest, then drew her finger lazily downward. "Besides, I'll bet there's more where that came from." She took me in hand, stroking slowly, at the same time spreading random kisses across my forehead, my mouth, my chest.

And I was ready once more.

And then suddenly hearing a sound, I was not. It seemed to

come from the kitchen, like a slipper on tile, and I rolled and reached down to the floor and touched the grip of my revolver.

"What's the matter?" she asked. Then without waiting for an answer she said, "It's nothing, it's just the refrigerator coming on."

I listened a moment. Hearing nothing, I returned to her, ran my fingers lightly over her nipples, then down across the dish of her belly, her hip bones coated in light from the hall, and she pulled me into her again, this time her movements measured, time expanding, the two of us barely moving, rising and falling in opposed synchrony for what seemed a very long, very heavenly time, and then she began moaning softly again, her movement quicker, her moans little cries, and I felt my loins surge and at the moment I exploded inside her the twilight of the room shifted somehow, and I twisted around to see a dark figure framed in the doorway holding a nickel-plated pistol. I rolled from her, still releasing, grabbing my revolver and a gunshot roared in a flashbulb of light. Eva screamed. Momentarily blinded, I fired at the doorway, twice, three times, and then I heard running, and a door slam.

I leaped from the bed, ran to the front door and threw it open. The gallery was deserted in both directions.

Naked, I closed the door, the light in Eva's bedroom coming on. Eva came into the bedroom doorway clutching a sheet to her chest, her other hand pressed to her mouth, her eyes wide with horror. I brushed past her, pulled on my pants and set about looking for a bullet hole around the head of the bed. It wasn't hard to find, about a foot above the headboard. Maybe he was a bad shot, or maybe it was a warning. But blood was boiling up my neck. I wanted this guy, and I wanted him dead.

I went looking for blood on the carpet, then on the tile floor in the kitchen. Then outside, walking the length of the gallery to the staircase at the street end, and back to the staircase that led to the parking lot. I hoped I'd hit the bastard, hit him good, hoping to find thick, dark puddles. But I found none.

The apartment walls must have been thick and soundproof. No lights came on, no one looked out. Back inside, Eva was sitting at the kitchen table in semidarkness. She had pulled on a bathrobe. Then I heard a car drive into the parking lot, followed by another, and I went to the bedroom, flipped off the light and peeked out between the blinds. Two squad cars were stopped in the lot below, their windows open, radios squawking on the night air. I rejoined Eva in the kitchen and flipped on the light, and a minute later the cops were mounting the stairs.

Eva looked up at me from the table, her eyes still frightened, but I wondered: Had she set me up? Was this an act?

The cops were rapping on someone's door. "Who do you suppose this guy was?" I asked her.

She shook her head slowly, her wide eyes riveted to mine. "I don't know, Mike. My God, I don't know!"

"Sure. Look, you better get some clothes on, the police will be here in a minute."

"I don't want to talk to the police," she said.

"What?"

"I don't want the police. We won't answer the door. We won't let them in."

"Right," I said. "Well, when somebody tries to kill me, I think I want to talk to the cops." I turned toward the door.

She grabbed my sleeve. "Mike, no, please." Half pleading, half truculent, she said, "This is my apartment, it's up to me. I say no police!"

I looked at her in disbelief. But I began to think: what good were the cops to me, anyway? I had no idea who the intruder was, and although I was pretty sure who sent him, I couldn't prove anything. The police would only complicate things.

I studied Eva's face. *Did* she set me up? I turned off the

kitchen light and went back into the bedroom and sat on the bed. Eva followed, closing the door behind her without a word. A minute later, the cops were knocking on Eva's door. Seconds passed. They knocked again. "Police, open up!" Then they banged on the door hard, and I saw, in the meager light from the window, Eva cringe and hug her knees. I sat there, waiting. After a couple of minutes their footsteps retreated down the staircase, and their cars pulled from the lot.

We sat there in the darkness without talking, maybe twenty minutes. Then I got dressed and let myself out.

CHAPTER TWENTY-SEVEN

I drove home tasting anger like copper wire in my mouth. A week ago, I'd let someone kick the crap out of me, and now someone took a shot at me. And like a hopeless drunk, I had fallen from my commitment to Beth without even putting up a fight. Where was I heading? Anger was building upon anger, dragged along by those triple catastrophes. Was I just going to take it from these guys? I tried a whole series of mantras: it isn't about you, it goes with the territory, it's not personal. When you take risks, sometimes the risks bite you. Get over it. Chalk it up, let it go.

But I never won any awards for self-control. In fact, for that reason I always felt a certain kinship with those fat people who are always dieting, yet will eat a whole box of donuts by tearing off one tiny little piece at a time. Knowing what's bad for you isn't the hard part.

When I reached my apartment the need for revenge had consumed me; the debate was over. I went straight to my sock drawer and found a sap, a flat blackjack with a heavy lead disk inside one end. I slipped it into my back pocket, then in the front closet found a camouflaged face mask I used for hunting. Then I drove to the Mt. Prospect apartment, parked in the shadows across the street from the apartment building and waited for the van from Earth Angels.

I must have dozed. When I opened my eyes the van was idling in front, the girls filing into the building. I couldn't see who was sitting behind the wheel, but since Tony trailed in behind the girls, I was pretty sure it was the Mexican. I pulled on the knit mask. When Tony closed the inner door behind him, I pulled across the street and double-parked next to the van, blocking it in. I went around to the driver's door and yanked it open.

"The fuck—?" That's all he said, the heavy sap slamming across his face. His head flew backward, blood spewing from his nose, and I grabbed the front of his jacket and dragged him onto the street. He fell to his knees and tried to cover his face, but I swung the sap again and again, his raised arms blocking some of the blows, but I landed a solid one behind his ear and he pitched forward onto the pavement. He laid there prostrate, very quiet. Too quiet. I bent, tentatively shook him. He didn't move. Then I knelt next to him, turned his face up and put my ear to his mouth.

He wasn't breathing.

"Oh, shit," I said, fear closing on my throat like a noose. I rolled him onto his back and lifted his shoulders and shook him hard, his head lolling like a stuffed animal's. He drooled. I put my ear to his mouth once more. Still not breathing—the blow behind the ear must have done it. Cold sweat covered my forehead. I'd wanted to hurt this guy, hurt him bad, but I didn't want to kill him. I let him slip to the pavement and then I pounded a fist on his chest, waited, and pounded again. I felt for a pulse. Nothing. And suddenly he let out a loud moan that made me jump, sucked in air and rolled onto his side. He raised his head and shook it and moaned again, as though that had been painful. He stayed in that position for what seemed like a long time, and then he turned on his belly and brought a knee up under him and tried to get up, but he wobbled and col-lapsed again.

I wanted to kiss him, but the sentiment didn't last long. He managed then to roll over and prop his back against the side of the van. I left him there, went to my car, to the pink paper bag on the backseat, and took out a set of handcuffs.

When I came back to him he was resting his head against the van door with his eyes closed, his face and the front of his jacket dark with blood. I snapped a cuff onto one wrist.

"What," he croaked. I lifted his arm and fed the other cuff through the door handle and closed it on his other wrist, and while he sat with his hands cocked above his head in what looked like some weird bird dance, I took my knife from my pocket and slipped the blade inside his waistband.

"No, please!" He tried to jerk away and sobbed, his nose full of blood, trying to shrink from the knife. I sliced through his belt and his pants and his underwear, then yanked them down around his ankles.

He cried out, "No! No!" Then he started screaming very loud, "Help me! Help, help, somebody please, HELP ME!" He must have thought I was going to bugger him. Lights started to come on in apartment windows.

"Shut up," I said. But I didn't want to hit him again. I walked back to my car and tossed his pants onto the backseat, then returning, I squeezed his face between thumb and forefinger, forcing him to look me in the eye.

"You are a message," I said. "To Stepan Vasil. Tell him: no one fucks with me."

I drove off then, and when I reached Algonquin Road I willed myself to drive slowly. Half a mile farther on, two squad cars zoomed in the other direction, lights flashing.

I drove directly to Club Belgrade. All the windows were darkened at that hour, but Stepan Vasil's Lexus was parked in the lot. I took the pants and noticed for the first time there was blood on them. Good, a bonus. I smeared blood on the windshield, then folded the pants under Vasil's windshield wiper.

Back in my apartment I noticed that my hands were trembling, and I poured myself a double Stoli, knocked it back while I stood at the kitchen counter, then I poured another and sat on the living room couch. Hands steadier now, I was still tossing on a sea of self-doubt, maybe the kind of emotion people feel in an earthquake, when the earth itself has no solidity. It was not fear of Stepan Vasil, or of the police. What terrified me now was my own demon breaking loose once more.

I finished the drink and poured another and sat down again, and when the Stoli delivered, like oil on troubled waters, a good measure of calm, I asked myself: can any good come of this? I'd sent a message to Vasil. I did it because the Mexican kicked the piss out of me, and then someone took a shot at me, and I could never, never let those things go. And because, though I was entering an age when men become candidates for bypass surgery, I had no more self-control than my dog.

CHAPTER TWENTY-EIGHT

The following morning I sat in my office window watching the scrawny trees along Washington Boulevard dipping their tops before an April wind, feeling a little better about myself. Maybe it was spring's eternal renewal; maybe it was just the daylight washing away the gloom of things I'd done in darkness. But at least the hair shirt of humiliation that had been forced on me was gone, replaced now with a humble sense of vindication. Well, maybe not so humble. And as far as my commitment to Beth was concerned, my Christian faith helped a little. Amazing grace: men fall, hope is eternal. I was probably a little like the Irish drunk who went through the Stations of the Cross backwards. Afterward he told the priest, "It was looking pretty bad for the lad, but I'm pleased to see he came out okay."

Those budding trees across from my window—their fragility, their invincibility—dredged up a memory, the cover of a book about the war in Bosnia. It was a grove of poplars, the bodies of several dead soldiers lying in a row beneath them, the trees just beginning to bud. The author, I remembered, was Terrence Bolt, a writer with the *New York Times*. Now I wondered: would Bolt have known any of the partners at Club Belgrade? Eva said they'd been major players in that war. It was a long shot, but I could try to contact Bolt.

On an impulse I called the *New York Times* and asked to speak to Terrence Bolt, afraid the operator would ask me what department he worked in. But she didn't hesitate. She transferred me to the foreign desk.

"Terry's away on assignment," the lady said.

"Can you give me his phone number?"

"Sorry, I can't do that. I can take a message, if you like."

"Look, it's important."

"Sorry, I'm not allowed to give out his phone number."

"Well, I can tell you he won't be happy if he misses out on this story."

"Does Terry know you?"

"Of course he knows me. And he'll want very much to hear what I have to tell him."

She hesitated, then said, "If you give me your name and number, maybe I can reach him. I can ask him to call you." Nothing ventured, I thought. I gave her three numbers: office, cell, and home.

Fifteen minutes later, Terrence Bolt called back. "You have some kind of story for me?"

"I read your book. It was astounding."

A moment of silence. "Okay." His tone was wary now. "Thank you. What did you want to tell me?"

"I'd like to ask you something. If you don't mind."

"Did you tell them at the desk that you had information for me?"

"Look, it's important. I'm a private investigator, and I was hoping you could help me."

"Mr. Duncavan—you know, I should really be pissed off, but then I guess I pull the same shit myself, sometimes. Okay, what do you want?"

"The war in Bosnia. Did you ever come across a guy named Stepan Vasil?"

"The Zipper? Sure."

"I think we cut out there a minute. What did you say?"

"The Zipper, General Vasil, that's what they called him. Why do you ask?"

"Long story, but he's part of a little enterprise I'm investigating."

"Vasil's in the states?"

"Yes. What can you tell me about him?"

Another moment of silence. "I had no idea he was in the states."

"What do you know about him?"

"He was a general in the Serbian Army. A really, really evil guy."

"What's with this 'Zipper' business?"

"That was his nickname, on account of his interrogation techniques. I should say, his *rumored* interrogation techniques. You know what a gutting knife is?"

"I think so. You mean a hunting knife with a hooked blade, for opening an animal's abdomen?"

"Right."

"I'm a deer hunter, I've got one."

"Yeah, well so did Vasil, only he used it on prisoners. He got a kick out of watching their faces when their guts spilled out around their ankles."

I hung up, fear like an icicle slicing up my back. I was in over my head, I had no plan, not even a next step, and I was very much alone.

I headed out to Monk's Pub, and though it was only noon, I ordered a double Stoli on the rocks and carried it to a table, drank about half of it before I took out a notepad and settled down to think. The police were not the place to look for help. The cops in the neighborhood drank cheap at Club Belgrade and surely regarded Vasil as their pal. That night outside the club, when I'd tangled with Wolfy and his goons, those cops were on me like yellow jackets at a picnic.

But maybe I wasn't entirely alone. Henry Verity was an ally of sorts, though that bond was at best tenuous. Could I tell him how I'd brought the whole business down to a personal level, how I'd nearly beaten that guy to death? Hell, I'd committed a felony, and something told me that Lieutenant Straight-laced would not approve. But then, there was really no need to tell him all the sordid details of my life.

I finished the Stoli, decided against having another, and wrote on my pad, "Call H. Verity." I underlined it once, then twice. Then I punctuated it with a big question mark.

I turned the page and wrote the name "Stepan Vasil" at the top and an arrow pointing from it to the words "Club Belgrade," then another arrow to the words "Demon Lover," then another arrow from that to the words "sex slavery." I stared at the diagram for a full minute, and found it so helpful I tore it up, crumpled it into a ball and dropped it in the ashtray.

So what did I have? Krunic gets his hand sawed off in a ritual murder. Eva has a prosthetic hand. Coincidence? Simunic was suffocated with a plastic bag. And a dead girl is found in the forest preserve, a plastic bag covering her head. Another coincidence? She's been dead for a long time, but then so was Simunic. There seemed to be, if not a pattern, a certain symmetry here. But even if it all shook down into some kind of M.O., it didn't point to the killer. One thing seemed fairly certain, though: whoever killed that girl in the forest preserve killed Simunic. Both got it about a year ago—same time, same method. So any progress the cops made in her case would point to Simunic's killer.

Did the same guy do Krunic? Exactly where he fit in, I didn't know, but probably.

I walked back to my office having decided to call Henry Verity, try to enlist his aid. I would tell him everything and take my chances—either he'd help me, or he wouldn't. I was pretty sure, if I made it sound like I was going to confession, he at least wouldn't turn me in.

I called from the office and reached Hank at home.

"Did you stay at the cottage?" he wanted to know.

"No, but I did drive in. Really nice place, I can see why you love it. Listen, we need to talk."

"Come by the house." When I hesitated, he said, "I'm off this afternoon, and I'm home alone."

We sat at his kitchen table. Hank popped the tops off a couple of Miller Genuine Drafts and without asking, handed me one. Though I thought I'd had enough at lunch, I took it. I told him first about meeting with Darryl at Celestial Bodies, that I thought that whole business was a dead end. He shook his head, gave me a skeptical look, but didn't say anything.

"What?" I asked.

"These people—what makes you think you can believe them?"

It took me by surprise. It wasn't what I'd come to talk about, and I was momentarily at a loss for words. "Can we kind of put that on hold for now? There's more."

I spilled it then, the whole story. Hank was a good listener, his expression sympathetic, he nodded now and then, never looked judgmental, and didn't interrupt me until I came to the part about getting shot at in Eva's apartment, and then only because I think I was a little vague in the details.

"Wait. Just so I understand—you were ah, in her bed when the guy came in?"

"Yeah."

"So she was—in the bed, too?" He must have caught the embarrassed shift of my eye, because he said, "I just mean, the bullet could have been meant for either one of you, right?"

"Right, but listen, that's not the end of the story."

I told him then how I'd nearly killed the Mexican with a blackjack, and how I'd delivered his pants to Vasil.

He sat back and pushed fingers through his hair. "Oh, shit," he said.

"Wait." Then I told him about my conversation with Terrence Bolt, and how Vasil had acquired "The Zipper" nickname.

When I finished, he said, "You want another beer?"

I nodded. He retrieved two more from the refrigerator, handed me one, sat down and said, "So what do you want me to do, Mike?"

I didn't have a ready answer.

He said, "Remember, I'm a tactical lieutenant in a district, this whole thing is way outside my league. And besides, you've still got nothing, evidence-wise. You don't know who took a shot at you, and you can't even make out a simple assault case against Vasil, not one that you can prove."

His eyes drifted off then, and we just sat there sipping beer, until a smile tugged at the corner of his mouth and he looked at me again. "Of course, with that ski mask they don't have anything on you, either—not that they can prove."

I shrugged.

"Hey, listen my friend, this is some bad shit. I mean the sex slavery thing, I told you that before. I could care less about the rest of it." He hesitated, his eyes searching mine, then in a quiet voice he said, "Listen, you know what this job has done for me? I know now in my heart that I could waste one of these mother-fuckers, just blow 'em away with a clean conscience. Go to Mass and Communion the next day, and feel virtuous about it. Sometimes I think the only thing that keeps me from something like that is the thought of going to prison. So believe me, I won't judge you for your, uh, lapse of judgment."

I looked him in the eye, wondering where he was going with this.

He leaned on his forearms. "You want my advice? Let it go, Mike. They hired you to find the murderer, but the Violent Crimes guys can't clear this thing, not with all their resources. And anyway, who cares if a couple of lowlife scum-suckers get their tickets cancelled? I'm sure you're a great detective, but the insurance company gave you an impossible job. And hey, it's not as if the insurance company's motives are pristine, either. They're just trying to get out from under their own obligation. If I were you, I'd send them a final bill, tell them you've done everything you can. There's no dishonor in that. Hell, that's just being square with them. Let it go, and you'll be out of this mess."

CHAPTER TWENTY-NINE

I spent most of the following day sitting in my office mulling over Verity's advice. He was right on every count. The case was, in the cold light of day, impossible, and I was just stealing the insurance company's money.

I turned to the computer, prepared a final report to Orson Prescott, detailing all that I'd learned, and in the last paragraph informed him that, regretfully, I'd reached a dead end. Then I went over it carefully, editing, rephrasing, cutting and pasting, and finally printed it out.

And then I crumpled it into a ball and pitched it into the wastebasket. There wasn't much to the report, but putting it together for the first time brought some things together like a stack of Lincoln Logs, and I thought I saw a faint ray of hope. If the suffocation deaths and the hacked-off hands were pieces to the same puzzle, Eva knew something about how they fit together. There might be a key to all this—the key under her doormat, if it was still there. Not sure whether she'd set me up, I hadn't spoken to Eva since that guy took a shot at me in her bed. That key was singing to me like a lovesick whale.

Eva usually started work about five o'clock, so I left the office early. An elevator repairman in freshly starched coveralls and a railroad engineer's cap was standing in the hallway outside my office, scribbling something on a clipboard. I said, "Hi." Probably accustomed to being ignored, he gave me a surprised smile and said, "How-de-do."

At this stage in life, I acknowledge all persons whom others fail to notice. Admittedly, the same people whom I too had failed to notice, in my life before I was disbarred and disgraced. After that, people who knew me took to casting their eyes elsewhere when I encountered them on the street. That changed me. As Beth, my ex, liked to say: "Out of every travail some good will come." Now I greet everyone—janitors, plumbers, street sweepers, window washers. I say thank you to crossing guards, and good morning to people distributing handbills on the sidewalk. Not that I'm Mother Teresa. But I've learned it's the small stuff that can make someone's day a little sunnier.

At home I found a flashlight in a kitchen drawer, slipped into the shoulder holster with the .357 Colt, and was going down the stairs when I stopped to consider. I was allowed to be armed while working, or when traveling to and from. I was working, and therefore could legally carry a concealed weapon. But I was about to commit a break-in, or at least a trespass. If I got caught, there might be the slimmest chance of talking my way out of it. But if I was armed, I'd be in deeper trouble. I went back up to my apartment and hung the revolver on the back of the closet door.

I got on the Kennedy at Fullerton, all lanes moving like a frozen river, inched along hoping that Eva's key was still under the mat. There was a good chance she'd removed it, since it seemed the only way the intruder could have gotten in that night. If he *was* an intruder.

I parked in the lot behind the building and climbed the stairs to the second floor without encountering any other tenants. Eva's curtains were open, the apartment in darkness. I rang the bell anyway and waited, *Hollywood Squares* blasting from a neighbor's TV. I rang again, gave it a decent interval, then lifted the doormat. The brass key swelled with light.

There were only three rooms—kitchen/dinette, bedroom, and living room. I closed the drapes, then went to the bedroom and flipped on the light. The room was free of clutter, the bed made. Opening each dresser drawer, I made a mental picture of the contents before moving anything. Nothing but sweaters and lingerie, all neatly folded. Her closet was packed with clothes, but everything was carefully arranged. I pulled down a hatbox from the shelf, which contained, surprise! A straw hat. I turned off the light.

Even with the drapes closed, I was afraid that lights going on and off might attract attention, so in the bathroom I shut the door behind me before flipping on the light. There were a couple of prescription bottles in the medicine chest, and towels were neatly stacked in a cabinet. Under the sink there were only cleaning materials and a hair dryer.

The first time I was here I'd been too preoccupied to appreciate how fastidious a housekeeper Eva was. Except for the choice of décor—modern, functional—the place seemed an exercise in Japanese minimalism. I didn't even find an errant piece of junk mail.

In the living room I switched on a desk lamp. The desk drawers contained only stationery, pencils, paper clips, and oddly, a bottle of ink and a collection of old fountain pens. There were no bills, no correspondence.

I left the desk lamp on and went to the kitchen, the light ample over the half wall, and examined the wastebasket. There was only an empty Cheerios box and the cardboard tray from a pork chop package. None of this told me much about the mysterious Eva, except that if she was Jewish she wasn't keeping kosher. Somewhere she had to keep bills, a checkbook, that kind of thing. The cabinets contained only dishes, glassware, pots and pans.

I'd nearly given up when I spotted it, on the top of a rounded shelf at the end of the cabinets, the corner of a shoe box stuck sideways behind a cookie jar. I took it down, opened it on the kitchen table. It was filled with rubber-banded packets of envelopes—bills, bank statements, the like. All were addressed to Eva at this address. There was nothing helpful. Then a photograph fell from between the last two packets and landed faceup on the tile floor. Reaching for it I froze, paralyzed by that face staring back at me. I picked it up and, trying to compute what it could mean, flipped on the kitchen light for a better look. It was a Polaroid shot, taken right here in this kitchen. A man looking over his shoulder from the open refrigerator, a surprised grin on his face.

The face of Henry Verity.

CHAPTER THIRTY

I crawled toward Bucktown on Northwest Highway, the city disgorging the dregs of the rush hour, wondering about that photograph. It should have come as no surprise, given that Eva tended bar at a club in Verity's district, that Eva and Henry would know each other. Nor should it come as a surprise that Hank might even have dipped his wick into the same warm place I had. Still—what were they to each other?

At Devon, the car ahead sped up to go through a yellow light and I started to follow, then the driver got cold feet and stopped. I slammed on the brakes, then braced myself with the sound of tires squealing behind me. In the rearview mirror, a dark Buick stopped an inch short of my bumper.

It wasn't until I reached my block and was backing into a parking space that I noticed a dark Buick waiting behind me. When I got parked and it pulled past, I had a sickening feeling it was the one that nearly hit me, that I'd been followed. McClean is a one-way street, and the Buick pulled to the curb on the opposite side in front of the school. Three men were in the car, two in front, one in back, and I sat there waiting for them to get out. But they didn't.

Sure now that they were watching me, I got out, walked over to the car and looked in the passenger side. I couldn't place the guy staring back at me. He didn't even have the courtesy to roll down the window. But I recognized Stepan Vasil, sitting in back, and the driver was the Mexican whose bare ass I'd last seen in my rearview mirror a couple of nights ago. Then I remembered the guy in the passenger's seat, still in those starched coveralls and engineer's cap. I was pretty sure he didn't know how to repair elevators.

"How-de-do," I said to him. He kept that blank stare. They did not seem in the mood to chat, so I gave them a friendly wave, which none of them acknowledged, and turned to go.

But I wasn't going to walk straight to my door, and tip them to where I lived. I made a decision, which turned out to be a mistake. A big mistake. I walked to the playground gate and started diagonally across it, knowing they'd be unable to follow in the car. But the sound of car doors slamming and footsteps hurrying in my direction set a bat loose in my belly. I was in trouble. Because of my bullet-ravaged ankle I could not run except for short bursts. So I stopped, turned to face them as they approached, black silhouettes against the streetlight. They stopped, their long shadows leaning toward me. And then a chromium spark leapt from something in the Mexican's hand, the curved blade of a gutting knife.

"Hey!" I yelled, as loud as I could. "HEY, CALL THE COPS!" That got them moving again. I turned and ran to a corner of the school, shafts of pain screaming up my leg, then around into an empty courtyard bisected by a triangle of light, trotted along the wall in the dark half, found a recess cut into the building and ducked in. I pressed my back against the bricks and waited, their footfalls drumming around the corner. They stopped. Somewhere a bus released its brakes. A horn sounded in the distance. Now their shoes scraped gravel, and the three walked right past me. Should I try to run for it? No, I couldn't outrun them.

They had passed my line of sight now. "Dumb fuckers!" It was Vasil. "Fucking morons, how could you let him get away?" Now their feet crunched gravel again, coming back my way. Vasil said, not so loud this time, "You know what, you stupid shits? I think I'll hire this Irish cocksucker. Forget it, I will kick your moron asses out, and I will hire the Irishman."

They came into view, the Mexican's head jerked around in my direction as though noticing the space for the first time, and then he looked me straight in the eye. "Hey!"

He was on me in an instant, and then the other one had my arms pinned behind me. They pushed me out into the open, toward Vasil.

"No, you assholes, keep him in there." They threw me back, arms locked behind me, pushed my face against the bricks.

Vasil said, "Now I'm going to show you, Mike Duncavan, why you don't fuck with Stepan Vasil. I'm going to show you what happens to amateurs who want to play big leagues. Antonio?"

The Mexican released my arm and the other guy took hold of both of them behind me and swung me around to face them. The Mexican moved close, the hand with the knife held down at his side, his body a silhouette against the light from the courtyard. "I told Antonio he could do this," Vasil explained, like it was some kind of deal he'd made for my benefit. "If he doesn't fuck it up, he can do it. Don't fuck it up, Antonio."

Antonio's knife arm seemed to stiffen. My butt puckered. But he didn't raise the knife, just stood there looking at me. I couldn't see his eyes, but thought that while Antonio lusted for revenge, he may not have been up to ripping a guy's guts out. That was, well, pretty gross.

For me, there was only one thing left to do: Yell my head off. "HE-EY!" I screamed. "HEY, POLICE! HELP, HELP, PO-LICE!"

"Do it, moron!" Vasil hissed.

Antonio's shoulders relaxed, a movement of resignation, and his hand came up uncertainly, like he was considering whether to start at my solar plexus and rip down from there, or maybe the other way.

And then behind him a silent figure slipped into the bright half of the courtyard.

"Mike, that you?" It was Fred Havranek, my landlord. The three men turned to look at him. He was standing statue-still, lances of chrome light shooting from the fire ax he held across his thighs. "The cops are on the way," he said.

CHAPTER THIRTY-ONE

Ten minutes later I was sitting in Fred's den with a glass of brandy in my hands, Fred standing on the couch in his socks replacing the ax onto its mahogany hanger. "Piece of shit wasn't made to be used. But then, for splitting heads, I think it would do." He shrugged and stepped down. "Hey, I wish I had something other than the brandy. You drink what, vodka?"

"This is fine," I said, and took another long drink, the fire steadying my hands.

"Guess I've turned into the neighborhood busybody in my old age, huh? I was actually watching out the front window when you parked your car. When I saw them following you, I was pretty sure it was trouble. But I never really did call the cops, Mike. I thought I'd better get right over there, not waste time on the phone. Shouldn't we call the cops now?"

I shook my head. "It'll only complicate things. Besides, what can I prove? They got three witnesses against one, and at most, it's a simple battery. And I take it you really didn't see them do anything."

"Fuck, one had a knife, didn't he?"

"I'm pretty sure he did, I really didn't get a good look at it."

"I make a good witness, Mike. I'll tell the cops whatever you want, just tell me what to say."

I shook my head. "I don't want you involved in this, Fred. But thanks, I owe you one. A big one."

"Listen, since I retired, the only adventure I get in my life is having you for a tenant."

I finished the brandy, said good night, and climbed the stairs to my apartment. The light was flashing on the answering machine in the kitchen. Three messages, all from Eva, each sounding more desperate than the next.

"Mike, please call me, it's important." She left her cell phone number.

Then, "Mike, please call me as soon as you get this message, I need to talk to you right away."

The last: "God Mike, please, please pick up the phone!"

She answered on the first ring. "Mike! Oh, thank God. I've got to talk to you."

"Where are you?"

"In a coffee shop across from Pal Waukee airport."

"You're not working?"

"I called in sick. Can you meet me right away?"

"Can you give me an idea what this is about?"

"How can you ask me that, after what happened the other night? I'm frightened, Mike. Very, very frightened."

She gave me the location of the restaurant. I took the Kennedy to I-94, got off at Willow Road. Eva had sounded scared silly. My suspicion that she'd set me up to get shot was beginning to dissolve, but not completely.

She was sitting in a booth at the back, and when she saw me coming her smile flashed like the airport beacon. Since she was facing the door with her back to the wall, I said, "Mind if I sit there?" Indicating her seat. It may not have been the chivalrous thing, but I wasn't about to leave the entire restaurant at my back.

Her eyes were bright and moist, and she lifted a hand to my neck and pulled me into a kiss, more joy than passion. "Thank you for coming," she said. Then she scooted over to make room, having misunderstood my lack of chivalry anyway. I slid in next to her.

"Mike, I'm really, really afraid. I think they want to kill me." Then she added, her eyes full of implication, "Since they know I'm—seeing you." Emphasizing the last words, making sure I got it.

Seeing you? I let it go and said, "Eva, you may think I know things I don't. Maybe you should just start at the beginning and tell me the whole story."

She pulled back, searched my eyes for a few seconds. Then she lit a cigarette. Sitting next to her, it was hard to see her eyes. I moved around to the other side of the booth. But she would not look at me, anyway.

"They brought me here from Yugoslavia," she said to the tabletop. "Like all the girls, they told us we had jobs waiting for us in United States. Nothing to worry about, they told us, they would take care of all paperwork, everything. And we don't even have to pay in advance. We pay back from what we earn." She brushed her eye with a finger.

"Funny, what you earn never really covers even expenses. You just keep getting deeper and deeper in debt to them.

"They didn't take us to the States, not at first. They took us to a small town in Mexico." She raised her chin a little, still not looking at me, her focus distant, tears welling in her eyes. "They beat us. They raped us. Over and over, they raped us, it was so, so, deliberate, so routine, they wanted to make us lose all respect for ourselves, our own bodies. They fucked us and they fucked us, until fucking didn't mean anything anymore. They told us that if we even thought of escape they would kill us." She fell silent then, finally turning her eyes into mine.

"Do you know if they killed anybody?" I asked.

"They killed girls, yes, but I never saw. I saw girls beaten, tortured, plenty of times. Sometimes, girl would just disappear."

Then she raised her prosthetic hand, and in a shaky voice she said, "Where do you think this came from?"

I shook my head and waited, hoping not to reveal how anxious I was to know.

She shuddered, put her hands to her face and began to weep. Then looking past my shoulder, her expression grew hard, like Kevlar plates sliding into place beneath the planes of her face. When her eyes joined mine again, they were dry.

"The body they found in the forest preserve, the girl with the plastic bag over her head? They killed her. A new girl, she just came up from Mexico."

I waited for her to go on. When she didn't, I said, "Who killed her, Eva?"

"Simunic," she said. "She was a tough girl, that one. They beat her, beat her horribly—but they couldn't break her. So they took her for a ride, Simunic in the backseat. That was the last time I saw her."

"Eva—did you see any of this happen?"

"No, I didn't really know the girl."

"Did you ever see her?"

"Yes. Her name was Camilla Orec. This much I know."

"How did you find out about this?"

"I heard about it." She shifted uncomfortably. "Jesus Christ, the girl is dead, what's wrong with you? You doubt it happened?" Eyes welded to mine, she shook her head in rebuke.

"Eva, please try to relax—"

She interrupted, stubbing out a cigarette. "I can't relax."

"What say we get a drink somewhere?"

"Sure, let's go," she said, and was out of the booth and walking to the door before I got to my feet.

We took my car, drove in a silence that gave me time to think. We had a lot of painful ground to cross, and alcohol tended to affect her emotional balance. But what the hell, I needed a drink, too.

I drove to the 94th Aero Squadron, a bar and restaurant made to look like a bombed-out French farmhouse, its complex of rooms filled with memorabilia of the Great War. We took a booth in a corner that gave us some privacy, and after the waitress took our order, I said, "I'd like to hear about what happened to your hand, Eva."

Absently, she ran a finger along the back of the prosthesis, then covered it with her palm and leaned toward me. "I was thirty-three years old when they brought me here. I was no kid, you know? I was professional dancer in Yugoslavia. Not a damned stripper, a professional ballerina. Thirty-three, that's getting a little old for dancing. So they came to me, and I fell for all their shit, walked right into it. They took me to that filthy Mexican place, forced me to fuck and suck whoever they wanted, whenever they wanted. They degrade you in every way, beat you for the slightest reason, make you completely dependent on them. And soon you are grateful to these pigs—grateful!—for any little kindness. And then—" her voice caught. She started to weep again.

I waited. When the waitress came over with our drinks, Eva sat up, composed herself, and with the waitress standing there, she snatched up her glass and knocked it back. "Bring me another one, please," she said. "And bring him another one, too."

I smiled lamely at the waitress. She smiled back, and when she was gone Eva picked up my glass. "Mind?" I shook my head, and she downed mine, too.

"They were good to me, really," she said.

Did I hear right? Her voice betrayed no irony. Then tears began to well again. "I mean, they decided I could help with the girls, to be a sort of a mother figure to them. You could say I played good cop to their bad cop." She searched my eyes looking for a sign of judgment; then it seemed, looking for forgiveness. "I got special treatment. No longer did they treat me like an animal. You could say, I became just like them."

"In Mexico?"

"In Mexico, yes, then up here. Some girls were suited to be dancers, those were sent to clubs. Others, they were strictly for sex. It was me who decided whether they could dance or not."

"You started to tell me about your hand."

Her shoulders sank and she stared at the table, not speaking for a moment. Then without looking up she said, "Stepan and I became lovers. I had my own apartment by then, near Club Belgrade."

"Were you working at the club then?"

She shook her head. "Not then. One day, when it was over between Stepan and me, I told him I was through with the whole business, I was leaving. They could kill me if they wanted to, but I was taking back what was left of my life.

"All three of them were there that day. I just went to my bedroom, threw some clothes in a bag and started to walk out. It was Milan who stopped me. He slapped me hard. Then he beat me. Stepan did nothing to stop him. They locked me in my room, and later I heard them arguing, a violent quarrel. I could hear very little of the words, but I knew Stepan was saying that they should not kill me. And I heard the other two saying to him, over and over, 'It's the only way.' Sometimes in an angry voice, sometimes pleading: 'Stepan, Stepan, it's the only way.' Then when it got dark, they came for me. They covered my mouth with tape, taped my arms also, and drove me to a forest preserve. Milan and two other guys, not the partners." She fell silent, her lower lip trembling.

When she continued, her voice was fragile. "They led me down a path into the woods, Milan walking ahead with a flashlight." Her eyes lifted into mine. "I walked along, you know? Willingly I walked, thinking only that it will be over soon. We came to a fallen tree. 'Here!' Milan said, and he pushed me to the ground. Then one of them cut the tape from my wrists while the other one held my arm across the tree trunk, and Milan brought the chainsaw." Her words cracked into a falsetto. *"He cut off my hand."*

She bit her lower lip. "Then one of the others wrapped my arm in a towel, and they put me back in the van. Milan said, 'If you open your mouth, next it will be your tongue. You should be dead. You should get on your knees and thank Stepan.'

"They drove me to a hospital and Milan waited in the van. He told me to say that I had been helping someone to cut boards with electric saw—table saw? And my hand slipped."

"And they believed that?"

"No, they did not believe it. The doctor was suspicious. They called police. The police questioned me, but I stuck to it. The police didn't believe, either. Next day detectives came and questioned me. Then after that more detectives, but I stuck to my story."

She lit another cigarette and, calmer now, she said, "One day, I just went back to them. Who would hire anyone like this, what could I do? Stepan took me back, was kind to me. They all were kind, really, considering. They gave me bartender job."

"Eva, you said they killed that girl, the one who was found in the forest preserve. How did you find out? I need to know what you can say firsthand, what you can testify to."

Her eyes went round. "Testify? Do you think I would tell anyone this? Mike, I have told you this because—because you got me into this, this situation I am in now."

"I *what?*"

"It was you that made Vasil angry. You made this vendetta

against him. You've got to help me, now. I don't know where else to turn."

"Vendetta? I didn't—"

She swatted the air. "No. You don't go to war with someone like Stepan Vasil. The man in my apartment last night, he must have followed you. And now—" She paused, weighing her words. "I'm afraid to go to work, I'm afraid to go to my apartment. When I called in sick today, Vasil came on the phone. He asked me where I was, called you my 'boyfriend.' 'Tell me, Eva, where is your boyfriend?' " Her eyes narrowed in accusation. "He told me about what you did, about what you left on his car. Now I don't know what they'll do to me. I have nowhere to go."

"Who killed Uri and Milan? You must have some idea."

"I don't. Swear to God, Mike, I don't, and neither does Stepan. Sometimes he gets crazy with it, trying to figure it out. All I know is, everybody who works for Stepan is wondering if they'll be next. He can't keep workers."

"Wolfgang?"

"Wolfgang wants out, I know that."

"Does Wolfgang help with, ah, enforcement?"

"No, he's just in charge of security for club."

"But he must know what's going on."

"I don't know what Wolfgang knows."

"Come on, how could he not know?"

"I'm not saying he doesn't know, he's just—I never really talk to him about any of it. Sure, he must know things. I know that Vasil confides in him now and then. But Wolfy's a clever guy, he does his job at the club, and doesn't want to know about the rest." She thought a moment. "A good German, you might say."

"What about Tony?"

"Tony's a different story. He's a bad guy, he's the enforcer, him and that bunch of scum that work at Demon Lover."

"Is Luis part of the scum?"

"Not Luis. I told you before, Luis is okay. Dumb, but really sweet. He didn't come up from Mexico like the rest, he grew up in Chicago, he only works with Wolfgang at Club Belgrade. Those others, they bring girls from the brothels in Mexico, and work with Tony up here. Strictly for Demon Lover." She hesitated. "They would kill me just for telling you this, you know?" She blinked and almost smiled, as though it was actually cathartic. "I've told you enough, you don't need to know any more. Now you need to tell me: what do I do now?"

I shrugged. "Eva, I don't know what you expect from me."

"I don't think it's safe to go to my apartment. Can I stay with you?"

She couldn't know about my adventure in the schoolyard, and I decided not to tell her. Vasil now knew the block I lived on, if not the house. Until now I'd been assuming they'd followed me to Eva's apartment that night, but now I thought they may have already been there, waiting for her to come home, and spotted me letting myself in. If that was the case, they would probably assume that she'd invited me. And that meant I had indeed put her further at risk. But I wasn't sure my apartment would be the safest bet.

"I'll get us a motel room for tonight," I said, expecting some protest.

But all she said was, "I'll need to get some things from my apartment."

"I don't think that's a good idea. It's just tonight. In the morning, we'll figure out where to go from here."

"Fine," she said.

CHAPTER THIRTY-TWO

I found a motel on Milwaukee Avenue, a hot pillow joint where the proprietor asked me how long I needed the room. I said, "For the whole *fucking* night," but he seemed not in the mood for wit. He gave me a weary look and insisted on payment in advance.

It wasn't until I closed the door behind me that prurience tingled my thoughts for the first time that evening, induced, probably, by the sight of the queen-sized bed and Eva slipping out of her jacket, her breasts lifting the pink shirt tucked into her narrow-wasted jeans. That brought a hard-on that would cut a diamond.

"Do you need to use the bathroom?" she asked.

I shook my head, and she went in and closed the door, and a moment later she had the shower running.

I slipped off my shoulder holster, hung it on the back of the chair, then sat on the bed with my back against the headboard, mental reruns of the schoolyard flashing through my head like a silent movie. I had seriously taxed my ankle when I tried to run, and after Fred showed up, I was forced to limp away from those goons like some wounded animal. They saw me as vulnerable. Surely now they saw me as prey. They'd be back.

In the short time it took to think this over, every trace of libido had fled my body, replaced with a growing irritation, followed by anger, and finally, getting to my feet and pacing the room, with fury. I could not hide here like some goat tied to a stake.

I slipped the shoulder holster back on and rapped on the bathroom door. "I'm going out," I said, and didn't wait for an answer.

I drove aimlessly for half an hour, finally decided to pay a visit to Club Belgrade. And then? I didn't know. This was a work in progress.

I should have used a credit card for dinner and the motel room. My wallet was about empty, so I stopped at home to pick up some cash, and while I was there I popped a handful of ice cubes into a glass, filled it to the brim with Stoli, and sat at the kitchen table. The Stoli had brought a little equanimity, so I finished and poured another three fingers and sat on the couch this time.

"Listen to your saner side, just this once," I said aloud. The sound of my own voice alarmed me; I really needed to calm down, to get my head straight. But I had to do *something,* couldn't just let things sit as they were and allow the goons to draw strength from that picture of me limping away on the school ground. The longer that impression lasted, the worse it was going to be for me.

I decided I'd go to the club but just not start anything—show the flag, have a drink, let them know I was still around. And see how the place was getting on without Eva.

I parked in the lot and walked around to the front. From inside the muffled beat of the music, more concussion than percussion, spread itself on the night air. Wolfgang and Luis were working the front door. Wolfy moved in front of me with a weary expression. Luis just stared.

"Where's Vasil," I said. "I'd like to talk to him."

Wolfy shook his head. "I got to talk to you," he said.

"Yeah? So talk."

"Not here, not now. Mike, don't make trouble for yourself. None of this is going to do you any good."

"None of what?" When he didn't answer, I asked him again, "Where's Vasil?"

"I told you. He's not here."

"You told me where he isn't. I asked you where he is."

"You want to go inside? Go ahead. You're behaving like a fool."

The DJ was ensconced on that high dais, the crowd on the dance floor swaying like a forest of kelp. In the bar, empty stools seemed hard to come by, but after half a circuit I found one. I didn't recognize the bartender, though considering the way he avoided me, I was pretty sure he recognized me. After he'd ignored me on the third pass and engrossed himself in conversation about twenty feet away, I walked over.

"You buzzed past me so many times, maybe you remember my face, I'm the guy sitting over there. I'd like a Stoli on the rocks." His eyes bounced away from mine, and I followed his gaze to the front door, to where Wolfy stood watching. Wolfy gave a small nod, and the bartender snatched up a glass, scooped it full of ice, and poured.

"Four-fifty," he said.

I started back to my stool but found it occupied and had to stand there, self-conscious now, an obstruction to anyone trying to pass, the bartender stealing frequent glances at me, and Wolfy staring from the door. After a while, weariness felt like a heavy yoke across my shoulders. What was the point of this? I reached between a couple of people at the bar, put down the glass and turned to leave, and then Wolfy was there in front of me. He leaned to my ear, trying to make himself heard above the noise. Or maybe, trying not to be heard by anyone else.

"I want to talk to you, alone. I'll come by your office tomorrow."

"Sure, I might even be there."

"Noon," he said.

Too bad I didn't leave a minute earlier, or maybe a minute later. If I had given that bartender a little more slack before confronting him, events would have lined up differently, and I would not have met Stepan Vasil as I rounded the corner into the parking lot. He didn't notice me at first, walking toward me from his Mercedes with his head down, his expensive leather jacket open to the warm night air, light splintering off several gold chains, and when finally he saw me his mouth opened a little and he stopped dead in his tracks. He closed his mouth and his expression remained deadpan, seemed at a loss for words. Behind him a couple of girls in high heels and short skirts were clopping our way. Vasil seemed shorter somehow, but also younger, more fit than I had noticed. I pointed to the chains at his throat. "Better stay away from the deep end of the pool with those," I said. Puzzled, he followed my finger, and then I patted his face hard. Not quite a slap, just a humiliation.

I walked around him and he screamed at my back, "You are a fucking dead man, Duncavan. You are fucking dead, you just don't know it yet!"

The clatter of high heels quickened, but I didn't turn around.

I started the long drive back to the motel. Then, really tired, I just turned my car toward home. The motel room was paid for. Eva would be safe there, with or without me. Maybe more so without me. But heading east on Armitage, I remembered she didn't have a car. So I kept going, got on the Kennedy, took it to I-294 and got off at Willow.

The motel room was in darkness when I pulled into the parking lot. I went in as quietly as I could so as not to wake her. I needn't have bothered; in the pale light from the open door, the bed was still made, the room empty. Eva's purse was gone.

I drove to the restaurant where she'd left her car. It was gone, too. I dialed her cell phone, got her recorded voice. I didn't leave a message.

Worried now, I drove to her apartment. Her car wasn't there, either, and her second-floor apartment was dark. I went up the stairs and knocked on her door. No answer. I lifted the mat. The brass key shone there, but I didn't pick it up.

I drove home, angst rising in my throat like indigestion. Please God, don't let her be kidnapped, don't let them take her. I pictured her bound and gagged, at their mercy somewhere, or cut up in bloody little pieces, and felt as helpless as if I was tied up myself. She'd been right, after all. Had she never met me, she would be happily tending bar right now, with no more cares than all the mopes lining the bar. I should never have left her alone in that room.

I reached my block ready to promise God I'd start going to Mass regularly, and then I spotted Eva's parked car across from my apartment, in front of the school, the orange flair of a cigarette inside.

I didn't even get my door closed when she stormed out of the car. "You shit," she said, and slapped me hard. It actually felt good, cathartic. I wanted to laugh. "Why did you leave me?"

"Better move your car." I pointed to the sign. "There's no parking after eight in the morning."

In my living room I put on Ella Fitzgerald, one of her favorites, and dutifully asked her if she wanted a drink, though in truth we'd both had enough. But then it seemed okay. In my relief at having found her, all problems seemed solvable.

She smiled, draped her arms around my neck, pressed that luscious body against mine, and turned with me in a slow dance.

"Vodka, please," she said, her voice like a stoked furnace.

But she never got that drink. There was something she wanted more.

CHAPTER THIRTY-THREE

Earlier that same evening, Lieutenant Henry Verity had been pulling out of Mama Baldacci's parking lot with an Italian beef and a sixteen-ounce Coke on the seat next to him when a call came over the radio. He'd skipped lunch and, now past dinnertime, he was really hungry. The call was a man with a gun in an apartment above a tavern on Milwaukee Avenue.

The dispatcher gave the job to beat car 1623, Officer John Menoni, a one-man car. Patrol Officer Smoot's voice came on the radio. "Sixteen-thirty-four's close by, Squad, I'll take it in."

Verity wasn't far away, either, and though the aroma of hot beef beckoned, he turned his car toward Milwaukee Avenue. He should at least drive by to see what was going on.

Thirty seconds later, the dispatcher relayed new information. "Sixteen twenty-three, it, ah, looks like the man may be holding a hostage in an upstairs bedroom, a little girl. Use caution." Henry picked up the microphone and said, "Sixteen-ninety going in."

Smoot was already standing on the sidewalk in front of the tavern when Verity double-parked, and as he walked over Smoot asked him, "Think we should go right up, Lieutenant?"

"Yeah." The two men started cautiously up the stairway, pistols held down at their sides, the air close and smelling of pot roast.

Above, a woman came out on the landing and screamed at them, "Hurry, he's got my daughter!"

202

They trotted to the landing and followed her into the living room. She turned to them with wide and fearful eyes and flung a hand toward the back of the apartment. "My God, my God, do something," she sobbed, "he's going to kill her!"

Verity went first down the hallway, both men pointing their pistols upward, to the open door of a back bedroom. Verity peered around the edge.

Bruno Malik was sitting on the bed in a sleeveless undershirt, his hair uncombed, his grizzled face unshaven, a little girl sitting on his lap. He had one arm draped around the little girl, his other hand resting on a chrome .38 Special revolver next to him. Malik stared at Verity with no expression, but the little girl looked at him with big, scared eyes, shuddered, lowered her head, and wept.

"Listen, sir," Verity said to him softly, "why don't you put the little girl down and we can just talk." He returned his pistol to his holster and took a small step into the doorway.

Bruno snatched up the gun, placed the muzzle to the child's head. "Get away," he spat.

Verity froze, but stayed in the doorway patting the air with his palms. "Okay, okay, I'm not going to do anything. See, nothing in my hands. Can we just talk?"

"Get back!" His gun hand flinched a little. The child wailed.

"Okay," Verity said, taking a step backward. "Okay, I just want to talk." His voice was calm. "Look, I got all the time in the world. Nobody's going to do anything, nobody wants to hurt you. Just tell me what's troubling you, and I'll listen, okay?"

He heard new footsteps coming in the front door. That would be Menoni. Verity desperately wanted to call for a hostage crisis team, but he couldn't take his eyes off this guy. Only seven, eight feet away—so, so close. Now the guy lowered the gun, set it back on the bed, kept his hand on it. Verity considered lunging. He decided it was too risky.

"What's your name?" the lieutenant asked conversationally. The man stared at him silently.

"Bruno," the wife cried from the living room. "Bruno Malik."

Bruno's face contorted. "Fucking cunt bitch!" he screamed.

"Bruno, calm down. I'm Hank Verity. This your little girl, Bruno?"

"No!" he spat. "No, she is not mine!"

"Look, I need to talk to the other officer here, for just a second. Okay?" Bruno just stared. "Menoni," Verity called out, keeping his eyes on Bruno.

"Sir." Menoni moved up behind Smoot.

"Tell the dispatcher everything is okay. Tell him what's going on, we're just talking, we don't want any more cars here. Tell him not to send any more *beat* cars, okay?" With the emphasis on "beat" cars, he hoped Menoni got the message—to call a hostage crisis team. Verity heard Menoni move back into the living room, then, heard him quietly tell the dispatcher that the lieutenant wanted a hostage team right away.

"Can we just talk now?" Verity said to Bruno, a little relieved.

"Talk? You got a gun, you want me to talk to you?"

"Sure, no problem. Look, I don't even want to touch my gun, okay? We're going to trust each other, okay?" He backed up a foot. "Now, Smoot here, he's going to take my gun out of my holster. Without putting his finger on the trigger. Real slow."

Smoot didn't move.

"Do it now, Smoot," he said, managing to keep his tone friendly.

Smoot moved up to Verity and took the pistol from his holster and stood there behind Verity.

"Okay, Smoot, you go back now," Verity said.

Smoot complied.

"Now," Verity held his hands up, palms out, spread his fingers. "How about you give up your gun, now, Bruno? So we're even?

Just push it onto the floor."

"Fuck you."

"Okay, Bruno, but I don't think this is fair."

"Tough shit."

"You don't really want to hurt this little girl, do you? Whoever you've got a beef with, it's not with the little girl, she didn't do anything wrong, did she?"

Bruno stared.

"You can't be the kind of a guy that hurts little kids, Bruno, even I can see that."

Bruno lowered his head a little. Then he squeezed his eyes shut, and a tear slipped from the corner of one eye. He kept his eyes closed, but his hand still gripped the revolver.

"If you'd just talk to me," Verity soothed, "I promise, we can work this out. If you want to keep your gun, fine. Just put the girl down, let her walk over to me."

Bruno's eyes came open, and Verity's heart sank. He should have lunged when his eyes were closed.

"I guarantee you, Bruno, there's better days ahead. Whatever's bothering you, it's only temporary. I know it doesn't seem that way now, but I guarantee it. Just let her go, and we'll take her to her mother."

Bruno's eyes widened and he screamed, "No! Her mother's a whore!"

"Then just let her come to me," Verity whispered. "Just let her come over here, I'll keep her right here with me."

Then from the other end of the hallway, his wife screamed, "Bruno, you pig! You rotten, filthy pig! Let her go!"

Bruno's face twisted into a grimace. "*I'm* a pig?" he yelled. He snatched up the pistol, raised it to the girl's head. Then with a frightful grin, he cocked back the hammer and yelled, "Okay, now you're going to see, cunt!"

There was no more time. Verity pounced, slapped the gun up

and away from the girl's head. It fired, and Verity grabbed Bruno's wrist, the two of them struggling, both gripping the gun. Smoot pulled the little girl from the room, and now Menoni lunged, the three men rolling on the bed in a death struggle. Bruno was strong, still had a good grip, the barrel shifting in increments toward Verity's face.

For just an instant, Lieutenant Verity looked straight down into the dark hole of the barrel. He never heard the shot, never felt the bullet enter his skull.

CHAPTER THIRTY-FOUR

I opened my eyes with the ringing of the phone, light sifting through the curtains, the red numbers on the clock at seven-fifteen. Eva stirred. I got up, went quickly to the kitchen so it wouldn't wake her, and snatched up the phone.

"Did you hear about Henry Verity?" Marty Richter said.

Still fogbound, I said, "What are you talking about?"

"Henry got shot last night. It's bad, he's in a coma. He's probably not going to make it."

A weight like an iron pig blossomed in my chest. I sank into a kitchen chair. "Do they know who did it?"

"Yeah. Verity walked into a hostage situation and tried to take a gun away from a guy who didn't want to give it up. It's in the morning papers."

I said goodbye, raced down the stairs, retrieved the *Sun-Times,* brought it to the kitchen table. The story was on the front page, and I stood at the table and read the whole thing. Henry was in critical condition at Northwestern Hospital. The article didn't say anything about a coma, but Marty probably had better information. I remembered from my days in homicide that a gunshot wound to the head usually started at critical and went south from there if it didn't kill you outright. Still, they weren't always fatal. Sometimes they weren't even serious. But a coma—that was grim.

Eva came to the kitchen door and yawned, clutching a sheet around her. "Good morning," she said. "I would kill for a cup of coffee." She came over to where I was standing, took my face in her hand and kissed me slowly, toying with my lips. Then she pulled back. "What's wrong?"

I had to think a minute. I never knew exactly what Verity was to her. "I just got some bad news. A friend of mine, a policeman, got shot. Maybe you know him." I watched her eyes. "A lieutenant, Henry Verity. He works at the sixteenth district."

It didn't require close observation. Her eyes grew wide. "Henry?" She pressed a knuckle to her mouth and slid into a chair. "You mean he's—?"

"He's alive, but it doesn't look good. It's in the papers." I slid the *Sun-Times* across the table. She stared at it, her eyes growing wet. After a while, I knew she wasn't seeing the words.

"You know him?" I asked.

She brushed her eyes with the back of her hand. "He was one of the detectives who came to question me, after—" She held up her prosthetic hand. "He was very good to me. Oh my God, Mike!" She put her face in her hands then, and sobbed quietly.

I put an arm around her shoulder, debated asking her exactly how good Henry had been to her. I didn't have to. After a minute she pulled herself together and told me.

"After I got out of the hospital, he came to my apartment to check on me every day. He even went shopping for me, and when I didn't have money, he brought me food. I never asked him to. He'd just come by and put it in the refrigerator."

"So you and Henry were—" I made a vague little rocking gesture with my hand.

"Were what?" She gave me a puzzled look, then said, "Oh, no, no way. Henry was wonderful to me, and I was very—I was fond of him. But he was married. Happily married. He really, really loved his wife. A very straightlaced guy, that Henry. He would never, never—" She shook her head, leaving the rest for me to fill in.

"Did you know he was once a priest?"

"Not a priest. He was in seminary, but never a priest."

I let it go. "And you never told him anything about the partnership? About Demon Lover, or what they did to the girls?"

"No, never. I told you, I never told the cops any of it."

"But Henry was more than 'the cops' to you, wasn't he?"

"Yes, he was, but I was afraid. I didn't tell anyone. And after they gave me a job, took me back, I—I couldn't do that to them." She gave it some more thought. "I couldn't do that to Henry, either, get him involved in that."

"You mean, you were still in fear of them?"

She sat back. "I don't know." She sat a minute, thinking. Then she said, "The truth is I was very, very much in love with Henry. But Henry was in love with his wife, there was no chance for me. Then after a while I couldn't stand seeing him, being near him. I wanted him so much. It was impossible. I decided I needed to stay away from him, for my own sanity. Which I did. Yes, there were times I was tempted to tell him everything, because I thought that would bring him closer to me, at least for a little while. But in the end, that is exactly the reason I never told him anything."

"You wanted a clean break?"

Tears welled in her eyes. She nodded.

"You're a strong person, Eva. I envy you."

"You envy me?" She smiled, blinking back tears. "I have never known a more strong-willed person than Mike Duncavan."

"Yeah, well, it isn't a strong will. Actually, it's just the opposite. I have as much self-control as your average barnyard animal."

CHAPTER THIRTY-FIVE

I didn't get to the office until about eleven-thirty that morning. I checked my messages and put on a pot of coffee, and it wasn't until the knock came to the door precisely at noon that I remembered Wolfgang Bauer's self-made appointment.

I swung the door open. He sauntered past me into my office and plopped himself in the chair in front of my desk.

I stood at the office door. "I've started charging a consulting fee, payable in advance. Sure you want to be here?"

"I'm sure you'll want to hear what I have to say," he said. "I've given Stepan Vasil my notice. I got my letter from the Police Department, I report to the police academy in three weeks."

He had my attention. I sat at my desk. "So why are you here?"

"Because I think you're a straight shooter, and there's some things you should know. Look, those guys are shits, but Stepan Vasil took care of me, and I'm not going to double-deal him. On the other hand—" He slouched in the chair, his tweed jacket falling open, revealing a pistol in a belt holster.

"You can get arrested for carrying that."

"I got a private investigator's license, same as you. You had yours a little longer, I checked with Registration and Education. Listen, Mike, you're a good guy and I'm not your enemy."

"Vasil is."

"Maybe you made him an enemy. But that doesn't make me

your enemy, especially now. I'm saying goodbye to that whole business."

"You seem pleased."

"I am not going to bad-mouth them. I am here to warn you, Mike. Look, my job was security at Club Belgrade, I managed to stay out of the other stuff. But I hear things. I heard what happened the other night, at that school. I think they just wanted to scare you, but—these are some bad motherfuckers, Mike. You should really back off before it's too late."

"That what you came to tell me?"

"Yes. Well, no. I did come to warn you, but I know it probably won't do any good. So there's a couple of things you should know about the murders."

"I'm all ears."

"First off, I don't know who killed the partners any more than you do. But there was a silent partner, Groan Jarni, in Bosnia. I know he contributed some start-up money, and he was supposed to become an equal partner. But he stayed in Bosnia and he never did anything else, and the other three partners decided he didn't deserve an equal share. I guess there wasn't much Jarni could do about that. Jarni wrote some pretty nasty letters. Threatening letters. Then—"

I raised a palm. "Wait a minute. You saw the letters?"

"Mike, I didn't come here to answer questions. But yeah, basically Jarni said that either he was going to be a full partner in the business, or there wasn't going to be a business."

"Then why doesn't Vasil suspect this guy?"

"He does, but he just figures that it wasn't likely that Jarni could reach them here, and besides, Jarni is still a partner, still getting some money, they just cut his share back to like ten percent. That's still a fair amount of money in Bosnia, so in the end Vasil figured he wouldn't really kill the goose."

"Unless he's somehow able to set up a competing operation."

"Not possible."

"Now that the others are dead, he still only gets ten percent?"

"I don't know that. I don't want to know anything about Demon Lover, and Vasil tells me very little."

I looked out the window, thinking a moment. For some reason, this Jarni wasn't listed as a beneficiary on the insurance policy—that left out collecting insurance money as a motive. Which still left a couple more motives, and members of this particular fraternity didn't seem to need a whole lot of reasons to kill people. "But—what's his name, Jarni, his letter did say that he's either a full partner or there won't be any partnership, right?"

"Yes, it did, and there's something else. There were notes, too, dropped off at the Club right after each murder. Stuck under the door during the night."

I turned back to him. "Notes?"

"Warning notes, two of them, both the same, one after Uri was murdered, the other after Milan got it. Five words: 'Get out of the business.' "

"That was it?"

He grunted.

"Do the police have the notes?"

"No, Milan and Stepan, neither of them wanted police involved."

"Then Jarni's probably here, in the states?" I asked.

"In Chicago, wouldn't you say?"

I stood, looked out the window again. This was adding a whole new dimension to everything. On the other hand, it could mean nothing.

"Forgetting Jarni for a minute." I sat at my desk again. "Why is Vasil so sure it wasn't someone else, some competitor?"

"No one's sure of anything. You've got to remember, my job was at Club Belgrade, so I don't know a whole lot about Demon

Lover. But Vasil did talk to me from time to time about the murders, trying to figure it out. He says it cannot be a takeover because there was no other communication."

"No offer he couldn't refuse?"

"Good way of putting it."

"So you really think Vasil doesn't know?"

"He has ideas, he'd like to know if Jarni's here, it's just that none of them fit. Since they killed Milan, he's been going crazy, trying to it figure out. What is the motive, who is it doing this. And people at Demon Lover are nervous, too, everyone's wondering if they will be next." He allowed himself a wry smile. "And then you come along, right in the middle of it. It's never a good idea to cross Vasil, but you picked the worst possible time for it. Listen, the main thing I came here to tell you is, stay out of it, Mike. You can still walk away. Otherwise, they will kill you for sure."

"Are you threatening me?" I watched his expression.

He didn't answer, just leveled his eyes and stared at me for several seconds. Then he got to his feet, put his hands on my desk, and leaning close said slowly, "Mike, fuck you." He turned his back and let himself out.

CHAPTER THIRTY-SIX

Wolfy was only gone about five minutes when Bill Spina called.

"Did you hear about Hank Verity?"

"Yeah, I did."

"Well, Ginny just called me with some good news. He's out of the coma and able to talk." He hesitated. "Listen, he's asked to see me, and I'm going over to the hospital. Want to come along?"

"Sure. You got a car?"

"No, I took the train in."

"I'll pick you up in front of your office."

We were outbound on the Eisenhower Expressway twenty minutes later, Bill sitting with his hands clasped in his lap, preoccupied with something. Finally, he looked over at me. "Got a little problem, Mike."

When he didn't go on I said, "What is it?"

"Ginny says that, ah, Hank wants the last rites."

I glanced over, not sure what he was getting at.

"I mean, he wants *me* to give him the last rites. Lord, I just don't know what to do."

"Is that—" I searched for a word. Kosher didn't seem to do it.

"Efficacious? Yeah. When you leave the priesthood they put you through this layification ritual. It's kind of like being drummed out. But they also tell you that you are forever a priest, at least in some respects. So if you're ever, say, at the

214

scene of a major disaster or something, you would still be expected to help out."

"I see," I said, although I wasn't sure I did.

"Lord," he said. "I don't want to do it. I don't think I should."

"I'm sure there are priests available at the hospital."

"That's the first thing I said to Ginny, but she said he was adamant, it was me or no one. Jesus, why me?" That might have been a prayer, so I didn't respond.

"Mike, when I called you I was really hoping you'd come with me so I could bounce this off you. What do you think I should do?"

There might have been three or four billion people in the world better qualified to answer that question, but here is the pearl I came up with: "I think you've got to do whatever you think is right, Bill."

He was quiet for a while, sitting in that rigid way. "Bottom line is," he said finally, "I don't see how I can tell him no."

"Then there's your answer," I said, sage that I am. "Don't you need—equipment of some kind?"

"Ginny dug out Hank's stole, she saved all that stuff. She brought his sick call kit to the hospital."

On the fifth floor the elevator doors opened, the odor of hospital ward carrying its reminder of the fragility of all of us. We paused at the door to Henry's room. Hank was propped up in the bed next to the window, Ginny standing at his side. Kevin, Hank's son, sat quietly in a chair in the corner. Spotting us there, Ginny put on a brave smile and came out, holding in her hand what I assumed was a sick call kit.

To me she said, "How good of you to come. Mike, right?"

I nodded. "I'm sorry, Ginny."

"I know Hank will be happy to see you. Maybe later?" I took that as a polite way of asking me to excuse myself. She looked at Bill a long moment, then without saying anything, she went back into the room and whispered something into Hank's ear. He craned around trying to look in our direction but couldn't quite make it. She went to Kevin, then, said something, and he followed her out of the room.

"Remember Mr. Duncavan?" she said to him.

"Yeah," Kevin nodded without looking at me. I had an urge to put an arm around his shoulders, but didn't. Then he turned without a word and walked down the corridor to a little circle of furniture at the end, and sat on a couch. He put his fists in his lap and studied his thumbs.

Ginny looked at Bill again, tilted her head in a silent question. Bill looked at me, then without a word took the sick call kit from her, went into Hank's room, and closed the door behind him.

"I'm going to the cafeteria," Ginny said. She waved to get Kevin's attention, gestured for him to come along, but he just lowered his eyes and shook his head.

When Ginny was gone I walked over to him, wishing the echo of my footfalls on tile didn't sound so ominous. "Your Dad is one terrific guy," I said. "There aren't many like him. He's tough, too. He'll pull through this, Kevin, you'll see."

Kevin nodded, not looking at me. I never was any good at this. I would have made a lousy priest.

I took a chair across from him, a dusty-green vinyl one that matched the couch. We sat there wordlessly for about half an hour until the door to Hank's room opened and Bill came out. Spotting us, he came over, a quiet fire burning in his eyes. I didn't know what it meant; he may just have been glad the ordeal was over.

"Hank wants to see you," he said.

"Me?"

"Yeah." He gave me a "dumb question" look, then walked

back with me to the door. Out of Kevin's earshot, he stopped. "He's gotten bad," he whispered. "I'm not sure how much he's—comprehending. Go ahead in."

I did, stood at the foot of Henry's bed so he could look at me without moving. His head was swathed in bandages, and what I could see of his face was obscenely swollen. His eyes were closed, his breathing slow and labored; he seemed to be asleep. One tube ran into his nose, another into his left arm, and a third into the back of his right hand. Then his eye that was not covered in a bandage came open. He stared at me blankly for a full ten seconds.

"Ken," he said. "Listen. The cabin."

"It's Mike Duncavan," I said.

"I know. Can you come closer, Mike?"

I moved up near his head.

"You know?" he asked. "You know, Kenny?" He struggled, each word like a boulder he was hauling up from deep inside. I didn't want to correct him again.

"The cabin, you know?"

"Yes," I said.

"The new shed? Please, please, Ken."

I was sure he was delusional. Then he said, "Ken—I mean Mike, sorry. What—? You were there, right, Mike?"

"Yeah, I was, Hank, you've got a lovely place there."

"Heaven," he said. "It's heaven. Listen, take care of it, Mike?"

Take care of his cabin? I didn't know what to say.

"Please, okay? Please, just say you'll take care of it?"

"Um, sure. Take care of what?"

"It's—the new shed, okay? Take care of that for me, please, Mike?" Desperation edged his voice.

"Okay," I said.

He began swatting the back of his hand against the bed rail, then, and I was afraid he was going to knock the tube out of his hand.

"What do you want?" I asked him. He turned his head and looked at the rail as though seeing it for the first time, then reached over it and seized my upper arm in a death grip. But he didn't say anything. Half a minute later, his eye closed. His breathing grew deeper, more relaxed, but he didn't let go of my arm. After a while, I released myself.

I took the Eisenhower to lower Wacker Drive, Bill sitting quietly, looking straight ahead, preoccupied. I had almost asked him how it went, a perfectly natural question under normal circumstances. But it didn't seem the sort of thing you asked a priest after he'd heard someone's confession. Or an ex-priest. And now he seemed so deep in thought I didn't want to intrude. When he finally shifted in his seat and looked at his watch, I took it as a signal and said, "Bill, Hank said something to me. Really strange."

"What was that?" he asked, not looking at me.

"He asked me to—I'm not sure. First, he asked me to look after his summer place. Or seemed to. Then he asked me—you know, he and Kevin built a new shed on the place last summer—he asked me to take care of the shed. Any idea what that's about?"

Bill shook his head slowly, eyes front. "Not a clue."

He didn't seem to want to talk, so I didn't say anything more until I pulled up in front of his building on Michigan Avenue. He shook my hand, gave me a wink and a smile. "Thanks, Mike," he said. He got out and walked into the lobby without looking back.

CHAPTER THIRTY-SEVEN

I opened the door to my apartment that evening and received a shocking surprise. Stapler, who was supposed to be with Beth, came charging at me, leaping and whining and trying to lick my face. Then I spied a note from Eva on a yellow legal pad on the kitchen table, and ice water filled my veins.

"I'm going out to pick up some groceries, be back about seven. A lady named Beth came by, said she was dropping off your dog. I didn't know you had a dog, but she really didn't seem in the mood to talk. Hope I did the right thing."

I dropped onto the couch still wearing my coat, gripping the note in both hands. My first instinct was to call Beth, to try to convince her that she'd probably gotten the wrong idea, finding Eva here. I could explain that Eva's life was in danger, that I was protecting her. But what would be the point of lying? I could tell Beth some of the truth, tell her that I was not in love with Eva. That was true. She just happened to be the woman I was diddling at the moment. I could tell her it was nothing serious, doesn't mean a thing. And I could make a kite out of a bathtub.

What I wanted most of all now was a serious drink, but even then I had trouble moving, the weight of the universe pressing me onto the couch. Stapler came over and dropped his chin on my lap. I sat there massaging his scalp until Eva came back. She didn't say hello, just set an armload of groceries and a sack of

Kentucky Fried Chicken on the kitchen table. Taking off her coat, she said, "I didn't know you had a dog. Did I do the right thing, taking him?"

"Yes, you did."

"She wasn't very friendly, that lady." I could feel Eva's eyes on me, prodding for an explanation. I didn't give her one.

A little while later, we sat at the kitchen table in greasy-fingered silence, working on the fried chicken. Finally, she said, "Something's wrong. Why don't you tell me who Beth is, and why she had your dog?"

I sat back. "She's my ex. She borrowed him for a while."

Eva wiped her fingers on a napkin and stared at me for ten seconds. Then she said, "She's very pretty."

I shrugged without looking at her. A minute later she got up, carried her plate to the sink, turned on the water and said, "I shouldn't be here, I can see that. I think I should leave." Hurt constricted her voice.

She had no right to be hurt. I slumped in my chair, too weary to think of the right words. "No, you need to stay here," I said.

"I'm going to get my things." She stalked into the bedroom, tears in her eyes.

I didn't need this. After a minute I followed her, not knowing what to say, found her standing in the bedroom with her back to me, and rested my hands on her shoulders. "Come on, Eva."

Her shoulders erupted in sobs under my hands. She shook her head bitterly and said, "You don't love me."

I was too astonished to respond. *Love* her? Where the hell did this come from?

She sniffled, but didn't move. "You've taken advantage of me, of my—my situation. You got what you wanted from me, didn't you? Well, go back to your wife, I don't want—" Now she faced me. "I'm leaving, I don't want to stay here one, more, minute."

I stood there, helpless, resentment boiling up in me. Angry, but also afraid. Eva seemed at the moment nasty and pathetic, a powder keg of instability. There was no predicting what she might do, and I craved to have her gone, to put distance between us. To reach out to Beth. But I couldn't allow her to leave. If anything happened to her, I'd carry that guilty baggage forever.

"You've got to stay here," I said. "Please stay, all right? I'll sleep on the couch." At the moment, I wished I could sleep in a different country.

She didn't answer for a long time. Then quietly, without looking at me, she said, "Okay."

I took Stapler for a walk. When I came back, the muffled sound of the TV was coming from behind the closed bedroom door.

For the next couple of days I would come home from the office and find Eva preparing a simple meal. We talked little, orbiting each other like a pair of binary stars, keeping our distance. Every day I tried calling Beth. I called the moment I reached the office, again around lunchtime, and before going home. In the evening, when I took Stapler out on his leash, I tried her on my cell phone. I left message after message asking her to call me, telling her that I could explain if she'd just let me, sometimes with a lump in my throat, knowing how feeble I must have sounded.

On the third day after Eva's outburst, I flipped on the six o'clock news and was startled by a close-up photo of Henry Verity's face filling the screen. It was a picture of him in uniform, and I knew instantly that he was dead. The reporter said he had slipped back into a coma, and had died quietly, then they cut to the Verity living room, a reporter interviewing

Ginny, who still wore her brave face.

I invited Eva to go with me to the funeral Mass at St. Juliana's, but she said no without giving a reason, and I was glad she did. I sat up in the choir loft, the only seating left, the congregation below a collage of black-clad priests and blue-uniformed police officers. Afterward, the pallbearers bore the casket down the church steps between two ranks of officers with white gloves and crossed batons, to the waiting hearse.

I rode with Bill Spina to the cemetery. Once again, Bill did not seem much in the mood for talking, so I made an ill-advised stab at levity. "They didn't ask you to say the funeral Mass?" I was instantly sorry I said it, and when he didn't respond I said, "Sorry, that was just plain dumb."

But Bill just smiled absently and shook his head. "I gave up the priesthood because of doubts of faith. The doubts have grown bigger, yet I'm feeling really guilty for doing the last rites. I really had no business doing that, breaking the rules. I think I committed a sacrilege or something. Weird how that should trouble me, huh?"

"You did what you thought was best." Recognizing a refrain from my lame advice a few days before, I added, "You followed your conscience, and you gave Hank what he felt he needed most in his final hour. What Ginny needed, and Kevin, too. What could be more Christian than that? Quit beating yourself up, Bill, there's no downside to what you did."

"I'm not a priest," he said, but after that, some of his fretting seemed to leave him. I resisted citing Catholic dogma, that a priest is a priest forever, but I had the feeling I'd said something he wanted to hear.

The cars from the cortege packed themselves bumper to bumper into a cemetery roadway. Near the tail end, we walked in the grass and warm sunshine to the top of a little knoll and took a place at the back of the gathering, under an oak tree.

The priest was intoning a passage from scripture, Kevin standing up there pressed against his mother's side, his eyes full of unbearable loss. Then after the priest closed the book, a few relatives and friends took turns recounting anecdotes about Henry, some of them humorous, some touching. There seemed to be a moratorium on mentioning Hank the priest, though.

That is, until Bill Spina left my side and made his way through the crowd to the front. "We should not hesitate to acknowledge Henry's labor in the vineyard of the Lord," he said. "He left a legacy, a spiritual endowment, one that remains with many of us whose lives he touched." His eyes scanned the group. "Henry left one very concrete legacy, which flourishes today: The Book Bag Program at Visitation Parish. I'm told that it's grown manyfold since Henry started it, and now it's providing books for many children whose families could not otherwise afford them."

Visitation—those yellowed spires above Garfield Boulevard reached into my head. It hit me like a sucker punch. My mind racing, the rest of Bill's remarks were lost to me.

I watched Bill making his way back up the slope toward me, stopping to shake a hand, exchange a word here and there. He seemed to avoid my eye. Then we walked back to his car in silence. It wasn't until he was pulling out of the cemetery gates that I said, "I never knew Henry was at Visitation."

"Yeah, I told you, remember?" There was something not quite natural in his tone. I couldn't remember him telling me that, and when I didn't respond, he said, "Hank was transferred there from St. Matthews, I told you that, that day at the Union League Club." His tone was more guarded now, artificial. Was I imagining it, or had a kind of wall risen up between us? This Giver of Last Rites had heard Hank's final confession, and he might have learned a great deal. The Visitation connection was a small thing maybe, but too strange, too coincidental, and I couldn't let it go. I started stringing it together, a montage of Henry Verity, bits of what I knew about him bobbing in my head like a tub full of Halloween apples. I saw again his strange irritation, that night at Frakes's fund-raiser, when the subject turned to the sex slavery business. Heard that anguished appeal just before he died, the summer cottage, that shed: *Please, say you'll take care of it?*

It was coming together, scraps joining to become bigger pieces, and then it hit me like a cold shower. It wasn't the shed. *There was something in the shed.* And I was pretty sure what it was.

Bill dropped me at the corner of Washington and Wells in front of my office, but when he drove off I didn't go up. I went straight to the Hotel LaSalle parking garage, retrieved my car, stopped at my apartment just long enough to pick up Stapler. I was grateful to find that Eva had gone out, and I didn't take time to leave a note. I'd call her later. I had a three-hour drive ahead of me.

CHAPTER THIRTY-EIGHT

The sun was just setting when I reached the sandy lane leading to the Verity cabin. From the lack of tire tracks, it appeared I had been the last one to drive in. I cut the ignition and sat for a minute listening to the ticking of my engine, and staring at the padlocked shed door. Weary from the drive, and its forced reflection on what I was getting into, I was no longer so sure of myself. Maybe my imagination and impulsiveness had once again joined forces to make a fool of me.

I got out, let Stapler gallop off to chew at tufts of grass among the jack pines, went to the rock under which the house key rested and lifted it. The key was still there, but I had no need of it. I carried the rock over to the shed, raised it up over my head, and brought it down hard on the staple that held the padlock. On the fourth try the padlock dropped into the dirt.

I swung the door open, the air heavy with dust and the odor of motor oil, and snapped on the light. A John Deere lawn tractor and two snowmobiles were crammed inside, and I scanned the work bench, with its rack of tools, against the far wall, the shelves. On the floor were coils of garden hose, unpainted birdhouses, a wheelbarrow, gardening tools stacked in a corner, and miscellaneous junk. But what I was afraid of finding wasn't there after all. I stood there a moment, amazed at the depth of my relief, wondering if Henry's strange request of me would forever remain a mystery. I turned to go, considering the grueling drive home in darkness, and reached for the light switch.

Then I spotted it, sticking out from a loft above the door. The grip of a chainsaw.

I took it down, carried it to the workbench, the plank floor creaking underfoot. For an old saw that had seen plenty of use, it was very clean. Too clean. I took a box wrench from the rack and removed the bar and chain, then probing with my pocket-knife into those recesses you never seem to reach when you clean a saw, I found what I dreaded: small bits of bone, black with old blood. Of course, it could have been animal bone. I'd seen farmers use a chainsaw to cut the hooves and antlers from a slain deer. But Hank wasn't a deer hunter. I knew without a doubt, this blood was human.

I thought for a long time about what to do with it, and in the end I just carried it to my car, lifted the hatch and laid it inside. I called to Stapler then, and when he jumped onto the front seat I closed him inside and walked back and secured the shed doors as best I could. Then I turned the Omni back down the long driveway and headed home.

With that mental legroom the long, open road provides, I reviewed the case, and saw now that I had unconsciously violated one of my own cardinal rules: Be careful about your as-sumptions. I had assumed that a single killer with a single mo-tive had killed all three—Simunic, Krunic, and that girl, Cam-illa Oric. An easy enough trap to fall into, but it was a trap nevertheless, and it had blinded me, kept me from spotting the symmetry of it all. It was like some baroque dance. Girl suf-focated with bag over her head; Simunic found suffocated with bag over *his* head. Eva, former ballerina, gets her hand cut off with a chainsaw. Then Krunic's hand is lopped off with a chain-saw. I bow to you, you bow to me. A kind of chainsaw ballet.

Hank's words, spoken at his kitchen table, fell into place like tumblers in a lock. *I know in my heart that I could waste one of these motherfuckers, just blow 'em away with a clean conscience. Go to Mass and Communion the next day and feel virtuous about it.* In his earlier life Henry probably believed, as do those gentler souls who eschew violence but pay others to carry their gun for them, that police work is brutalizing, that it steals your compassion. A word Hank wasn't afraid to use.

So when did Father Verity's epiphany come? When did he learn that the soul of a copper, helpless against the daily horror, silently screams with the pain of compassion? When had Father Hank discovered his way to ease it? He knew the partners killed that girl. He knew they suffocated her with the bag over her head, and he knew he couldn't do anything about it. He'd discovered, as most coppers do, that there was no balm in Gilead. So he killed Simunic the exact same way Simunic had killed the girl. He sent them a message—a message they couldn't decode. When they took Eva's hand, he sent another one. But even those "get out of the business" notes were too subtle. None of this made Hank a bad guy, not in my view. It was really kind of poetic. Besides: there but for the grace of God goeth yours truly.

Hank claimed he'd been on furlough the night Krunic was murdered, said he'd been staying at the cabin with his family. It was probably true. Hank didn't mind killing bad guys, he just didn't like to lie. Allowing for time to drive back to Chicago, stop at the police station and call for Smoot to come in—who at the station would have noticed Hank there?—then time to drive to Club Belgrade, do Krunic, and drive back to the cabin: six hours, tops. He'd be back in time for breakfast.

Though Henry had an aversion to mendacity, Eva could not have been altogether truthful when she said she'd never told Hank about what happened to her hand, or about Demon Lover's sex slave enterprise. Of course she told him—he knew.

I wondered: Should I confront her about her lie? But that would mean letting her know what *I* knew, and the last thing in the world I wanted now was Eva as a coconspirator. She must have suspected it was Hank all along, and knew that if she told me that Hank knew of her ordeal, that he knew all about Demon Lover, the truth would have lit up in my brain like a big neon finger that pointed directly at Henry Verity. So Eva protected Hank. She'd been resolved to protect Hank at whatever the cost. And I was resolved to keep Kevin from ever knowing any of this about his father.

I rolled through the O'Hare toll plaza and merged into the lanes of the Kennedy, remembering that I never told Eva I'd be gone a while—it had been a long time since I had to report my comings and goings to anybody. Stapler never answered the phone, and anyway his concept of the passage of time was pretty rudimentary. I dialed my home number. No answer. I dialed Eva's cell phone, got her answering machine, and after the beep I told her I'd be home by eight. Got off at Armitage and parked near the bridge over the Chicago River. When no one was around, I walked back and tossed the chainsaw over the railing.

When I got home, Eva wasn't there. I fed Stapler and let him out in the yard, retrieved a frozen pizza from the freezer, and while it was baking I left two more messages for Eva; one on her cell phone and one on her home answering machine. I poured a Stoli and watched the news, then opened a bottle of Merlot and ate the pizza in front of the television. With Stapler curled at my feet, I dozed off.

CHAPTER THIRTY-NINE

When the phone woke me I was sitting upright on the couch with an awful crick in my neck, the luminous numbers on the VCR at three-fourteen. I staggered around looking for the portable phone. The answering machine clicked on, but whoever it was had hung up. I found the phone on the night table in the bedroom, and left it there.

A little more awake now than I wanted to be, I nevertheless got into my pajamas, and was just crawling between the sheets when the phone rang again. This time I got it on the first ring.

Stepan Vasil said, "Hey, Irish, we got your girlfriend here, why you don't come pick her up?" Before I could answer, he said, "Here, I let you talk to her."

"Mike?" Eva said, her voice breaking with terror. "Don't listen to them. Don't come here."

"Eva, where are you?" Then came the crack of a palm striking flesh and Eva screamed.

Vasil shouted, "I *told* you, cunt!"

Vasil was back on the line. "We are at the club, and we're waiting for you. We just want to talk a little, that's all. She won't get hurt if you come now. Otherwise, who knows what could happen? Just park in the lot. Be sure you come alone, Irish, and knock on back door."

"Listen, shit-for-brains, I'm sending the cops over there right now."

"Good idea. They will pound on door and no one will answer,

and then tomorrow Eva will be gone and you can be sure there will be no witnesses to anything except maybe to your sick imagination. Come right now, and come alone. And no weapons, Irish."

He hung up. I sat on the edge of the bed, the phone still in my hand. It was Monday night, the club was closed. Vasil had it wrong—I could meet the police at the club and tell them they were holding Eva. They wouldn't just walk away. Depending on how convincing I was, and on the disposition of the copper who showed up, they'd bang on the door, and chances were pretty good that if nobody answered, they'd break in. I dialed 911. But then what? It was a good bet that by that time Eva would be nowhere to be found—and might never be seen again. I couldn't say for sure that Vasil was a cold-blooded killer, but he was definitely a killer.

On the other hand, he might not be planning to kill me. Maybe he just wanted to rough me up a little. I could take that. This was real life, not some cheap detective story, and guys like Vasil didn't kill for no reason. But had I given him reason enough? He wanted revenge; would he really go that far? Wolfy said that he'd only been trying to scare me, that night in the schoolyard. Maybe I could just humble myself, make a plea. Maybe he'd be satisfied with just hurting me a little. If it meant freeing Eva, for once in my life I could hold my hat in my hand. I owed her that. I'd chalk it up to character-building.

I dressed in a hurry but when I couldn't find my shoes I grabbed a pair of moccasins from the closet floor, and as I slipped them on an idea hit me. I had a little Browning .25 caliber pistol, even smaller than those little chrome-plated ones women in noire films pull from their clutch bags and shoot from the hip. It was so small I used to carry it in my uniform watch pocket, the butt tucked behind my leather belt. Strictly a belly gun, but the magazine did hold six shots—and with a round chambered, seven. I could conceal it in the palm of my hand; would it fit in my shoe?

I found it in my dresser under my socks and checked the magazine: full. I tucked it into the heel of my moccasin, slipped the moccasin on, and took a few steps. It induced a definite limp. I slipped it out, noting that the thickest part was the grips. With a small screwdriver I removed them, and tried it again. I still limped, but less obviously. Then I remembered: Last time they saw me, in the schoolyard that night, I was limping. It probably wouldn't raise any suspicions.

I put the gun in my jacket pocket and drove to the club, intending to slip it into my shoe when I parked in the lot, but turning onto Belmont I realized that a welcome committee might be waiting in the parking lot, so a block from the club I pulled over and slipped the gun into the heel of my moccasin.

There were three cars in the parking lot: Vasil's Mercedes, the blue Buick, and a beat-up Dodge van. I knocked on the side door—the one through which Milan Krunic made his final exit. In the symmetry of this odd ballet, did the door hold the same ominous significance for me? I knocked again, filled with a temptation to walk quickly to my car and come back another time, preferably in daylight.

Then the door swung open and Tony was standing there, the phony elevator mechanic behind him. He grabbed my arm, yanked me inside, slammed the door, then walking fast he shoved me ahead of him across the barren dance floor. Real amateurs—there were a dozen ways I could have spun and taken him down. I really didn't think the paunchy one was much of a threat, either. So far, they'd showed no weapons. But these were the kind of guys who probably didn't get far away from them.

They halted me in front of a steel door, and the paunchy one swung it open, onto a dimly lit staircase to the basement. Tony shoved me hard and I stumbled but steadied myself on the hand-rail, then he shoved me again, and this time I stumbled and nearly fell, and as I swung my leg to catch my footing, the weight of the pistol sent my shoe flying. It landed upside down on the basement floor. As far as I could see, the pistol was still inside. I made my way quickly down the rest of the staircase and bent to pick it up, but Tony, who apparently didn't see the shoe come off, shoved me ahead of him again, and I turned to see the portly one start to bend to pick up my shoe. I assumed—I hoped—the pistol was still there and I jerked away from Tony, snatched it up and tried to pull it on, feeling the pistol lodged in the toe. Tony came for me with fire in his eyes, but the portly one said, "Relax, okay? Just let him put his shoe on."

I sat on the bottom stair, tipped the pistol back into the heel, and slipped my foot inside the moccasin.

"Come on, get the fuck up." Tony helped me to my feet with a little more enthusiasm than it required.

The basement was damp and broad and open, the light from a single bare bulb at one end glowing on ranks of beer and liquor cases stacked along one wall. Yellow light was leaking around a door which was open just a crack. The fat guy rapped softly on the door, then pushed it open.

Vasil sat in the small room, glowering behind a desk, a military-style nine-millimeter pistol in front of him, pointing my way. It wasn't until they pushed me all the way inside and shut the door that I saw Eva sitting behind it, her wrists duct-taped to the arms of a metal chair, a silk scarf tied around her mouth.

"Did you search him?"

The two eyed each other dumbly.

"Fucking morons! Search him!" Vasil shouted.

I extended my arms, palms up. Tony pinched along my sleeves, then up and down my flanks, then along my pant legs, and when he grazed my crotch I said, "Oo-ooh, I think I love you."

It was a mistake. He cracked me hard with an open hand across the mouth, rattling my jaw and teeth. I tasted blood. My head rang.

I must have telegraphed something of the pain to Vasil. He sat back with a satisfied grin and said, "You know, I kind of like you, Irish. So you make me sad, what you make me do. You give me no choice. Nowhere else to go with this."

"What do you have in mind?"

He snickered. "First, you will watch what happens to someone who double-crosses me." His eyes shifted to Eva. "We deal with her first, then you."

And then he astonished me. His eyes came back into mine filled with torment, his voice nearly cracking. "I gave this woman everything," he said, seeming to fight back tears, and it astonished me. He was still in love with Eva. "Do you know the many ways she betrays me? What else can I do with her?" He looked at her again, but when she joined his gaze he looked quickly to Tony and commanded, "Do it."

Tony took a folding knife from his pocket and opened it, exposed a long, serrated blade. He grabbed a handful of Eva's hair, tugged her head back, and put the blade to her throat. Eva let out a muffled sob, tried to shrink from the blade, but Tony held her fast.

And then came the sound of footsteps trotting down the stairs. Tony released her hair and looked over at Vasil, whose eyes were angry now. The footsteps crossed the concrete floor, and Tony started for the door when it swung open. Wolfgang Bauer pushed past him, Luis behind him.

"The FUCK you doing here," Vasil shouted.

"Stepan, let them go," he said.

Vasil was on his feet. "You don't belong here, neither of you.

Get out of here." Luis, eyes big and uncertain, stood in the doorway behind Wolfgang not saying a word.

"Stepan, please," Wolfy said, his voice surprisingly plaintive. "Please, you won't get away with it. Let them go." Then before Vasil could answer, he said, "Stepan, I'm doing this for your own good." He took a knife from his own pocket, ran the blade in one quick gesture under the scarf behind Eva's head. It drifted to the floor, and Wolfy bent to the task of cutting the duct tape from her wrists.

He didn't get far. Tony grabbed the front of his shirt and shoved him away, Wolfy falling against Vasil's desk, and Tony lifted his knife to Wolfy's throat.

And then Wolfy did that amazing pirouette, his foot connecting with Tony's head almost too fast for the eye to follow. Vasil's hand went for the gun, but Tony fell against the desk, knocking it away. I kicked off my shoe, snatched up the pistol, slid the safety off. Vasil was on his feet now, swinging his pistol toward Wolfy. I straight-armed the .25 against Vasil's head and shot him twice, his head jerking violently, then whipped the gun toward Tony, lying on the floor. He wasn't moving. I swung the muzzle into the fat guy's cheek. He held his head rigid, trembling. "No, no, don't shoot, don't shoot."

But my finger was closing on the trigger. I couldn't hear him. It was Wolfy's restraining hand that stopped me. "Mike, no, don't do it. It's over."

CHAPTER FORTY

It *was* over. Eva told her story to the Violent Crimes detectives, and Violent Crimes called in the FBI. Facing serious jail time, Tony sang like a contralto, spilled everything about the operation, gave up his Mexican counterparts, who joined in the chorus to the Mexican authorities. The Mexican police raided the brothels and set free a lot of women who, seeing the empire crumbling, were eager to testify against their captors. The lights at Earth Angels went out, and as far as I know, they never came on again. Last time I drove by, the building was boarded up.

I knew the whole thing might turn into a major news story, but never thought it would make headlines all over the country. Orson Prescott called me two days later, before I had a chance to give Piedmont Mutual my final bill. I sensed that he was displeased.

"Let me get this straight, Mike," he said. "I hired you because we didn't want to pay out another million bucks on this life insurance policy. So you go and you, uh—" He seemed to have trouble formulating his thoughts. Then voice shaking, he shouted, "You *killed our insured?* Have I got this *right?*"

"I think you're oversimplifying it, Orson," I said, holding the phone away from my ear. "Basically, I guess that's right, though. Yeah. It was self-defense."

"You charged us a hundred bucks an hour. I got this big bill sitting right here in front of me. And you think we're going to *pay this?*"

"That's only a partial bill. I should have the final one to you by the end of the week."

"Mikey, I wouldn't hold my breath."

"Orson, better talk to your manager before you do anything rash. Remember, he thinks I have a winning way with juries. I'll sue your asses off, and I'll ask those twelve good and true for all those fees you screwed me out of on my first bill."

"You can't even practice law, you disbarred, disgraced—*fuck!*"

"Yeah, but I can represent myself."

"YOU COST US A MILLION BUCKS!"

I hung up.

But I never did send the final bill. I walked over to Monk's Pub at noon that day and, rewarding myself, suspended the no-drinks-before-five rule. In the serenity of the second Stoli I arranged and rearranged the ethical issues like a stack of Legos. The company had, after all, hired me to find the killer. I'd done that. But on the other hand, I couldn't tell them who the killer was, so I could not ethically take their money. It did, in the end, come down to a matter of ethics. I thought of it as a tribute to Henry Verity.

I never saw Eva again. Club Belgrade was closed for a while, eventually opened under new owners. It kept the name, but without Eva. I don't know what happened to her.

The sweetest thing to come out of it all was a call from Beth, a surprise early one morning as I stood in my office window watching platoons of Loop secretaries pass in review. The sound of her voice, neither friendly nor hostile, put a lump in my throat. "I've been reading about you in the newspapers," she said.

"I really, really miss you, Babe." She'd caught me off guard, and it just escaped. I sat down, clutching the phone as if it might get loose, wishing I hadn't said it.

"Yes, well, the woman in your apartment, the one with the

prosthetic hand—she was the one you were protecting?"

"Yes," I said. I wanted to say a whole lot more, but the words would not come.

"Those—those gangsters, Mike, they actually cut off her hand?"

"Yes, they did."

"How horrible, I just can't imagine." Then: "Are you okay, Mike? I mean, God—what you've been through."

My gut melted. "No, I'm fine." Taking a shot at levity I said, "I got a million dollars' worth of publicity." I really wasn't sure that was true.

She hesitated. "Is that—that woman, is she all right, now?"

She was fishing, I thought. "I don't know, Beth. I haven't seen her, I have no desire to see her. I don't know where she is." Was I protesting too much? I nearly added, *and I don't care,* but that might have sounded callous.

"Well—I'm glad you're all right." Then tenderly, "I worry about you, Mike."

"You do?"

"How could I not."

"Then have dinner with me. Tonight." That escaped, too.

She didn't answer for a long time, which made me realize I was holding my breath. Then she said, "No."

"Can I possibly change your mind?"

"Mike, Mike, Mike. What good could possibly come of it?"

"What harm? Just say yes, don't think about it. I'll drive out tonight, pick you up."

In the silence, I could hear my own pulse. "Bring Stapler, okay?"

We had dinner in a romantic little Italian place in McHenry with white tablecloths and candles on the tables. Afterward, I stood on her front porch like a nervous teenager and kissed her good night. She kissed me, too, held nothing back. Then she said good night, and quickly went inside.

We keep in touch. I talk to her on the phone once in a while, and during idle moments, I still stare at her picture sitting on my office credenza. Maybe some day—I don't know.

About a year later, I was taking a shortcut through Marshall Field's and the woman behind the perfume counter looked over at me. Our eyes met—she was beautiful, perfectly groomed, her frilly blouse buttoned at the throat, lime-colored jacket hugging the curve of her body, black, shiny hair framing dark, familiar eyes like parentheses. It was Opal. She looked nothing like a Moravian farm girl, never mind a stripper. The last time I'd seen her, she was wearing that appalling bruise on her face, and called me a creep. Now her smile was warm—affectionate?—as if she wanted me to linger.

But I didn't. I looked away, not entirely sure she recognized me. She could have just been turning her company face to a potential customer. But I like to believe it was a smile of recognition, maybe even gratitude. It's one of those impressions you like to keep.

ABOUT THE AUTHOR

A Chicago native, **Thomas J. Keevers** is a trial lawyer and former homicide detective with the Chicago Police Department. *The Chainsaw Ballet* is his third novel in the Mike Duncavan series. He has published a number of short stories, one of which, "Thanksgiving Day in Homicide," was anthologized in *New Chicago Stories* and featured on National Public Radio's "Stories on Stage."

The father of four, he lives in Park Ridge, Illinois, with his wife, Rae, and his hunting dog, Star.